I pressed my body flat against the ground, desperately trying to bury myself in the tall grass surrounding me. The horses' hooves thudded along the dirt road, the sound allowing me to drag in several noisy gulps of air without fear of detection—at least from breathing. The horses did not gallop but walked slowly, inexorably toward me, toward my hiding place.

A full moon shone down on me, highlighting my pale-pink cotton blouse to anyone who cared to search the meadow. I didn't know how the riders hadn't spotted me before now. If they had, wouldn't they have called out to me? Alerted the others that some sort of pink creature lurked in the grass? A pink troll? A leprechaun? Wait! Wasn't that Ireland? They didn't have leprechauns in Scotland, did they?

I was losing it. I just knew I was. I had to pull myself together and fight against the hysteria that threatened to engulf me.

Since I had awakened on the riverbank, I'd been wandering for hours and hours in the dark. It had been midafternoon when I fainted—or whatever had happened to me after I splashed a bit of icy Highland water on my face—but dark when I awakened. I wasn't sure how long I'd been unconscious. The dizzy spell had taken me by surprise, and I had no idea what had caused it.

As I had drifted along the path, the moon had come and gone, often hiding behind clouds, and I'd lost any sense of direction. I hadn't heard the hum of the river for some time, and I didn't know when I had left it behind.

Any normal person might have thought I would have welcomed a party of riders, that I would have cried out to them for help. I had just been on the verge of doing that, when I heard their voices, their words.

My Laird's Heart

Bess McBride

MY LAIRD'S HEART

Copyright 2016 Bess McBride

All rights reserved. Without limiting the rights under copyright reserved above, no part of this publication may be reproduced, stored in or introduced into a retrieval system, or transmitted, in any form, or by any means (electronic, mechanical, photocopying, recording, or otherwise) without the prior written permission of both the copyright owner and the above publisher of this book.

This is a work of fiction. Names, characters, places, brands, media, and incidents are either the product of the author's imagination or are used fictitiously. The author acknowledges the trademarked status and trademark owners of various products referenced in this work of fiction, which have been used without permission. The publication/use of these trademarks is not authorized, associated with, or sponsored by the trademark owners.

Contact information: bessmcbride@gmail.com

Cover art by Tara West
Formatted by Author E.M.S.

Published in the United States of America

ISBN-13: 978-1535404693
ISBN-10: 1535404698

Books by Bess McBride

Time Travel Romance

My Laird's Castle
(Book One of the My Laird's Castle series)

My Laird's Love
(Book Two of the My Laird's Castle series)

Caving in to You
(Book One of the Love in the Old West series)

A Home in Your Heart
(Book Two of the Love in the Old West series)

Forever Beside You in Time

Moonlight Wishes in Time
(Book One of the Moonlight Wishes in Time series)

Under an English Moon
(Book Two of the Moonlight Wishes in Time series)

Following You Through Time
(Book Three of the Moonlight Wishes in Time series)

A Train Through Time
(Book One of the Train Through Time series)

Together Forever in Time
(Book Two of the Train Through Time series)

A Smile in Time
(Book Three of the Train Through Time series)

Finding You in Time
(Book Four of the Train Through Time series)

A Fall in Time
(Book Five of the Train Through Time series)

Train Through Time Series Boxed Set
(Books 1-3)

Across the Winds of Time

A Wedding Across the Winds of Time

Love of My Heart

Historical Romance

Anna and the Conductor

The Earl's Beloved Match

Short Cozy Mysteries by Minnie Crockwell

Will Travel for Trouble Series

Trouble at Happy Trails *(Book 1)*

Trouble at Sunny Lake *(Book 2)*

Trouble at Glacier *(Book 3)*

Will Travel for Trouble Boxed Set *(Books 1–3)*

Trouble at Hungry Horse *(Book 4)*

Trouble at Snake and Clearwater *(Book 5)*

Trouble in Florence *(Book 6)*

Will Travel for Trouble Boxed Set *(Books 4–6)*

Trouble in Tombstone Town *(Book 7)*

Trouble in Cochise Stronghold *(Book 8)*

Trouble in Orange Beach *(Book 9)*

Trouble at Pelican Penthouse *(Book 10)*

DEDICATION

To all my loyal readers who love the combination of
time travel romance and the mystique of the Scottish Highlands!

Here is another one for you!

Dear Reader,

Thank you for purchasing *My Laird's Heart*. *My Laird's Heart* is book 3 in the My Laird's Castle series of Scottish historical time travel romances set in the aftermath of Culloden. The dialogue is laced with what I hope is enough Scottish dialect to give the reader a historical feeling, but not quite so much as Robert Burns might use such that readers have to reference their Scots-English dictionaries throughout. As I did. I hope you enjoy the story of Lily and Calum.

The years following Culloden have taken their toll on the Highlanders. Few who participated in the Jacobite rebellion survived, and of those who did, some have either escaped Scotland or gone into hiding.

Lily Brown falls into the same time travel void that Beth Pratt and Maggie Scott did before her. But she isn't rescued by a laird as her predecessors were. No, a secretive and enigmatic Highlander with no apparent fortune or title finds her lost in the eighteenth century.

Beth Pratt and Maggie Scott fell in love with their lairds and gave up everything to stay with them. But Lily Brown can't imagine spending the rest of her days in eighteenth-century Scotland or with a Highlander who keeps his secrets.

Thank you for your support over the years, friends and readers. Because of your favorable comments, I continue to strive to write the best stories I can. More romances are on the way!

You know I always enjoy hearing from you, so please feel free to contact me at bessmcbride@gmail.com or through my website at http://www.bessmcbride.com.

Many of you know I also write a series of short cozy mysteries under the pen name of Minnie Crockwell. Feel free to stop by my website and learn more about the series.

Thanks for reading!

Bess

Chapter One

I pressed my body flat against the ground, desperately trying to bury myself in the tall grass surrounding me. The horses' hooves thudded along the dirt road, the sound allowing me to drag in several noisy gulps of air without fear of detection—at least from breathing. The horses did not gallop but walked slowly, inexorably toward me, toward my hiding place.

A full moon shone down on me, highlighting my pale-pink cotton blouse to anyone who cared to search the meadow. I didn't know how the riders hadn't spotted me before now. If they had, wouldn't they have called out to me? Alerted the others that some sort of pink creature lurked in the grass? A pink troll? A leprechaun? Wait! Wasn't that Ireland? They didn't have leprechauns in Scotland, did they?

I was losing it. I just knew I was. I had to pull myself together and fight against the hysteria that threatened to engulf me.

Since I had awakened on the riverbank, I'd been wandering for hours and hours in the dark. It had been midafternoon when I fainted—or whatever had happened to me after I splashed a bit of icy Highland water on my face—but dark when I awakened. I wasn't sure how long I'd been unconscious. The dizzy spell had taken me by surprise, and I had no idea what had caused it.

As I had drifted along the path, the moon had come and gone, often hiding behind clouds, and I'd lost any sense of direction. I hadn't heard the hum of the river for some time, and I didn't know when I had left it behind.

Any normal person might have thought I would have welcomed a party of riders, that I would have cried out to them for help. I had just been on the verge of doing that, when I heard their voices, their words.

"The men are weary, Lieutenant Dunston. I believe the village is not far now. It will do them good to rest in a warm building for the night after the rigors of the past week." The speaker's voice was deep, raspy. He sounded older, perhaps middle aged. His accent, while British, held none of the charming Scots brogue I had heard over the past month since I'd been in Scotland.

"I am largely unconcerned with the grumbling of men who cannot march above fifteen miles in a day or sleep on the ground for extended periods, Sergeant Wilson." The lieutenant spoke with a clipped English accent.

"Yes, sir. However, it must be past ten o'clock. I think it will do you good as well to rest and take some sustenance, sir."

When I first heard their words, I thought I'd run into some sort of military formation on a late-night exercise, though the sound of the horses' hooves and jingling of livery startled me. Did British soldiers still use horses for military maneuvers? The sergeant's next words dropped me to my knees, and it was then that I found myself flat on my stomach in the grass.

"We have been scouring the area for Jacobites for days on this patrol, sir," Sergeant Wilson continued. "I fear you will fall ill again if you do not rest."

"And what am I to tell the commander if the rebels he charged me to hunt down slip past us and escape Scotland?" the lieutenant asked. "What shall I say to him if Lord Malcolm Anderson gets away? I feel we are so close, that he is within arm's reach...if we expand our search, if we are more vigilant. No, I have no time to rest."

"With all respect, sir, you must. The rout at Culloden was almost complete, leaving only a handful of Jacobites to escape. If Lord Anderson remains in the Highlands, we will find him in good time."

Jacobites? Culloden? What?

There was a moment of silence before the lieutenant spoke.

"Yes, you are right, Sergeant. Patience is not one of my virtues. I would just as soon capture this 'laird' and return to the fort. In fact, I would rather return to England, where the hills are gentle and the air soft. We will stop for the night at the village. I'll take a room at the inn, and you will see to the men. Perhaps quarter them in the stables. They should be comfortable and warm enough."

"Yes, sir."

I lifted my head and peeked up through the grass. The moon, out for a brief moment, shone on two soldiers riding horses and about twenty men marching along behind, toting what looked like incredibly long bayoneted muskets. Their tricorn hats, long-skirted coats and light-colored leggings gave the surreal impression that they had just popped out of a historical movie.

No, not possible. I hadn't strayed onto the set of a historical movie! Where were the lights? The crew? The cameras?

My heart pounded as I lowered my head and pressed my cheek down against the grass, thankful yet again that the thud of the horses' hooves and men marching masked the short gasps for air I couldn't control.

Was this a dream? If so, it seemed very real, real in the sense that the ground was hard, the blades of grass sharp against my face, the night air cold. The day had been warm, and I had left my jacket in my rental car.

The sounds of the group faded, all too slowly, and I lay still for a few more anxious moments after I could no longer hear them. I lifted my head up and looked over my shoulder but saw no more of them in the darkness.

Instinct told me to run in the opposite direction, but self-preservation and a whole lot of confusion about my predicament told me to follow the group. The sergeant and lieutenant said they were heading for a village. Maybe I could find someone there to help me, someone to tell me where I was and how to get back to the car I had left in the view pullout above the river.

I pushed myself to my knees and then into a cautious hunched-over position, as if anyone who cared to look in my direction couldn't see me. I supposed I thought that if I stayed low, I might be able to dive back into the grass again if need be.

I could see nothing in the dark, could hear nothing, and I cursed myself for letting the group get too far ahead. How was I going to find them? I couldn't even see my own two feet at the moment.

The moon must have heard me, because it popped out from behind a cloud and lit up the meadow and the path that I'd traveled, the one that had paralleled the river until it coursed away. I hurried over to the path and turned in the direction the soldiers had gone.

As clouds threatened to block my precious moonlight again, I quickened my pace and practically trotted down the path. Forced to slow on several occasions when I could no longer see, I sprinted when I could.

The sound of men's voices caught my ears, and I stopped short.

"I'm tired as tired can be," one man grunted. "When are we going to stop for the night? Surely, we're not going to march all the way back to Fort William, are we?"

"Stop yer whining, Griswold," another man said. "It won't do you any good, and yer hurting my ears."

Clearly, I had come upon the men at the end of the formation, probably the only ones who could complain without being overheard, without retribution.

I wasn't quite sure how to follow the group without being able to see them. What if I moved too quickly and bumped into them? The men at the rear had fallen silent. I heard their footsteps and the occasional jingle of the horses' livery, but I couldn't gauge the distance between us. I hung back for a few moments, then hurried forward when the noise faded.

We traveled that way, my soldiers and I, for the next hour. Griswold continued to fuss, and his companion continued to berate him for doing so. Silently, I joined Griswold in fussing. How much longer were we going to march? I had already traveled miles since I'd awakened on the river, probably in the wrong direction.

I'd been squinting in the darkness, trying to concentrate on the uneven rutted trail while avoiding following the soldiers too closely, when I noticed a small yellowish light bobbing somewhere up ahead. A flashlight?

"Who goes there?" A gravely voice with a pronounced Scottish burr called out, loudly enough for me to hear him all the way in the back of the formation.

"Halt!" someone called out. I stopped obediently and froze in place.

"Lieutenant Dunston and Sergeant Wilson from Fort William," the sergeant called out. "Are you the night watchman?"

"Aye," the man said. "That be what they call me."

"My men and I need shelter for the night," the lieutenant called out. "I will take a room at the inn. The sergeant and twenty men will bed down in the stables or whatever else you have that is suitable."

"Ye can apply to the Blackbriar Inn. Just down the road. I watch out for the village at night. I dinna provide room and board and such. That be the business of the innkeeper." The light started bobbing again, as if the watchman moved away.

"Insolent buffoon!" the lieutenant snapped. The sergeant attempted to placate his boss with a few soothing murmurs. The horses moved forward, and the soldiers followed.

I waited a few moments, studying the bobbing flashlight or lantern of the watchman to see which way he went. I presumed by night watchman, he meant security guard.

One would have thought I would have run toward the guard for help—to ask him where I was, the location of the nearest telephone, how to get back to the pullout, back to my car.

But I didn't. Nothing about the verbal exchange between the watchman and the soldiers seemed normal to me, the entire conversation sounding fantastic and dreamlike…as if I'd wandered into a place that was lost in time.

I gave myself a shake and stepped out carefully, unsure of my footing as the moon hid behind clouds once again. Thankfully. I wasn't quite ready to reveal my presence in the very odd scene.

I stumbled a few times but recovered. I didn't know what kind of terrain the path paralleled, but the brief bits of landscape I'd seen in bursts of moonlight showed we had followed a trail that meandered through a valley and meadows such as the one that I'd hidden in. I hadn't heard the river for some time. Had we moved away from it?

The security guard's light disappeared from view, and I froze. Where had he gone? I peered into the darkness and listened intently. I couldn't see anything, but I heard noise up ahead, voices, some shouts.

"Here! See to these horses," someone called out imperiously. The soldiers! Apparently, they hadn't gotten too far ahead of me.

"Aye, sir," a young voice snapped.

"Where is the innkeeper, boy?" I recognized the lieutenant's voice.

"Inside, sir," the boy responded. I was close enough now to hear the jingle of the horses' livery, their snorts.

Oddly, I could hear the activity yet still couldn't see anything in the darkness. I moved in the direction of the voices but tripped and fell flat on my face in tall grass, with a grunt. Somehow, I'd lost the path. I jumped up and looked around.

As if the path had taken a sharp turn, soft yellow lights shone in the first- and second-floor windows of a building to my right. I couldn't make out the details of the building, but a door opened to reveal more lighting within.

I assumed we had arrived at the Blackbriar Inn. Exterior wall sconces highlighted the bright-red tunics of two men as they passed through the door.

The flickering lights also showed a short person, probably the boy, leading two horses away from the front of the building. The rest of the soldiers followed in the boy's wake, rounding a corner of the inn to disappear from view.

I hurried toward the near side of the building and huddled against the wall in the shadows. As if I were the lead character in a spy movie, my heart pounded with the covertness of my actions. I drew in a deep breath and peered around the corner toward the front door.

The path, now lit by the inn's exterior lighting, revealed itself to be a road in actuality, showing deep ruts, as if wheeled vehicles regularly traveled along the unpaved road. I could now see the outlines of several other buildings in the village, though all appeared to be dark.

The inn appeared to be the hub of the quiet village. Occasional bursts of shouts and laughter emanated from the building. Clearly, someone was having some sort of celebration, probably in a pub.

A pub! What better way to find some help! I squared my shoulders, took a deep breath and forced myself to head for the front door. I didn't care whether I'd fallen into a historical reenactment or what. I needed to make a phone call.

I passed a paned window and looked in. As I had suspected, it was a pub, albeit as bizarre as the rest of the night had been. Groups of people sat at long wooden tables centered by oil-burning lamps and candles. All seemed to wear some form of historical dress, the men featuring neckcloths and the occasional tricorn hat, the few women sporting ankle-length dresses and décolletages showing cleavage.

I caught sight of the lieutenant and his sergeant as they settled themselves at the end of one of the tables. The man I assumed to be the officer, by the epaulettes on his shoulder, was slight and short statured. He wore a white powdered wig, while the older sergeant eschewed such for his own gray ponytail.

One of the women, middle aged and plump, wearing a mobcap, grayish bustier and equally gray skirt over impossibly wide hips, delivered two tankards to the lieutenant and the sergeant. In looking around, I realized that the other two women in the pub were waitresses as well.

"What are ye doing, lass? How dare ye present yerself in men's clothing?"

I whirled around as someone grabbed my arm from behind. A short, stocky man wearing dark-brown trousers, matching coat and a tricorn hat over a stringy ponytail held me with one hand and hung on to a lantern with the other.

The security guard! He wore no official uniform but dressed as the men in the pub did, in historical clothing.

I wrenched my arm from his hand.

"Hey!" I snapped, somewhat from indignation but mostly from fright. "Take your hands off me. What on earth are you talking about? Who are *you*?"

"I watch over the village at night, lass. I dinna ken who you are either. Ye dinna live hereabout, but yer costume is in poor taste. Hurry home and put on some decent clothing." He paused and eyed me, quirking a bushy gray eyebrow. "And fer that matter, stay home. The inn is no place for a single lass at night."

I drew in a deep breath, still struggling with the surreal quality of the events around me since I'd awakened on the bank of the river. The old night watchman wasn't helping.

"Look, I'm lost. I must have fainted down by the river. When I woke up, my rental car was gone, I couldn't even find the pullout where we'd parked, and it was pitch dark. Do you have a cell phone?"

The night watchman stared at me and was on the verge of speaking, when the front door opened. The sergeant stepped outside and turned toward the wall, fumbling with his trousers as if he was going to relieve himself against the wall.

"Hold there, Sergeant! Ye have company!"

The sergeant, clearly startled, jerked and looked toward us. His eyes widened as he looked at me, and he dropped his hands to his sides.

"Who is this, watchman?" he barked. "Your daughter? What sort of costume is that?"

"Nay, Sergeant. This young lass is nay kin of mine. I found her outside the inn, as ye see her."

The sergeant approached, and I took a step back. Dark-brown eyes in a weathered face eyed me from head to foot. I shoved my hands in my jeans pockets and stared back as boldly as I could.

"Look, you guys. I'm just looking for a phone. I don't know what you have going on here. Frankly, I think it's a bit creepy, but if you just let me use a phone, a mobile, I think you call them, I can make a call and just be on my way."

The men exchanged glances and turned to look at me.

"You do have mobile phones, don't you? Or even a landline? I know this town seems kind of small and remote, but surely you have a telephone somewhere, right?"

"I dinna ken her strange speech, Sergeant."

"Nor I, watchman. I think you should see to her though. She does not seem well. I must return to my ale."

When the sergeant turned away, the night watchman reached out and grabbed his arm. The watchman had a bad habit of grabbing arms.

"Nay, sir. She came in yer wake, of that I am sure. She must have followed yer soldiers into the village. It is ye who must do something with her. I am fer my bed."

And with that, the night watchman stalked off. I watched him with wide eyes before turning to the sergeant. No matter what game these two were up to, I needed a phone. I spoke up again.

"You guys are really peculiar, you know that? I don't even know what to think. How about a phone? Or is there a woman I can talk to? How about the owners of the inn here?"

I stepped past him and wrenched open the door of the inn, startled at its heaviness. I stepped into not a lobby but the very pub I'd been watching. All eyes turned on me, and everyone fell silent. From the universally shocked expressions on their faces as they studied my blue-jeaned legs, I realized that something very, very odd, something quite extraordinary, had happened to me.

CHAPTER TWO

"What have we here?" the lieutenant drawled, the last calm note as a cacophony of voices erupted. The sergeant rushed in behind me, trying to grab my arm. The waitress I'd seen through the window rushed up to me.

"Here, lass. Ye canna be in here. We dinna consort with the likes of ye. Get ye gone now," she barked as she faced me with her arms akimbo.

"Wait! I'm just looking for a phone," I said, my voice drowned in the shouts, hoots, hollers and general noise of the room. One would have thought I was a tiger escaped from a circus and sauntering into the pub for a treat.

My heart pounded. In fact, it hadn't stopped pounding for the last half hour or so. No, maybe even the past few hours since I'd awakened by the river.

I was fast losing hope that there was going to be any rational explanation for the historical clothing that everyone wore, just as I wasn't going to be able to provide an explanation for the clothing that I wore—apparently equally as shocking to them as theirs was to me.

No one came forth with the offer of a phone. Weirdly still, no one raised their phone to take a picture of the commotion in the room. It was that small detail that convinced me beyond a shadow of a doubt that no one in the room had a phone. I couldn't imagine the remotest island in the Pacific without at least one mobile phone in this day and age. No, I had dropped into some sort of time warp. The only question was…when?

I turned to the sergeant, the man whom I'd actually known the longest in the room, all of about two whole minutes.

"What year is it?"

"What year?" the waitress barked. "What nonsense is this? Go now, lass. Go home, wherever that be."

"No, wait," the lieutenant said sharply. "Bring her here, Sergeant."

The waitress swung around to eye the lieutenant.

"Sir, we dinna take kindly to her sort at the Blackbriar Inn," the waitress began. The lieutenant held up a delicate but authoritative hand, and she pressed her lips together.

"As ye wish," she said resentfully with a dark look in my direction. She whirled around and hurried away toward a door at the back of the room.

The sergeant led me to the table and seated me across from the lieutenant. I seemed to have no will of my own. The brief spark of backbone that had galvanized me to rush into the building had vanished completely. I was lost, and not just in location either. I suspected I was lost in time, and that horror rendered me helpless. The sergeant could move my bewildered self around like a puppet.

"Where do you come from, girl?" the lieutenant asked. "You are not Scottish, I think."

On closer inspection, the lieutenant appeared to be about thirty. The tomato red of his jacket emphasized the pallor of his skin, almost as white as his wig. Prominent cheekbones dominated a clean-shaven face. Thin, almost bluish lips didn't smile but didn't frown either. Delicate pale-green eyes, albeit bloodshot, regarded me with curiosity and a hint of suspicion. Blue veins rose prominently in his hands.

"The States," I said quietly.

The sergeant took a seat beside me, straddling the bench to face me.

"The States?" Lieutenant Dunston repeated with a lift of one slender sandy-colored eyebrow. I assumed his hair was blond beneath the wig.

"America?" I tried.

"The Colonies?"

I nodded. Sure, if that was what he wanted to call them.

Over the lieutenant's shoulder, I noted a man with a dark beard and shoulder-length curly dark hair sitting alone at the table behind us. Although most people in the pub openly stared at us or threw sideways glances in our direction while vocally pondering my presence, the man sitting alone at the table behind the lieutenant was all the more noticeable because he appeared to ignore us. He kept his head lowered and slightly tilted so that his hair covered half of his face.

A dark-gray tam was pulled low over his forehead, ending just above thick dark eyebrows. His black overcoat covered broad shoulders. He toyed with a tankard of liquid, keeping it near his mouth without drinking. He looked up once, and I caught his dark eyes. He blinked and lowered his gaze again.

The pub had settled down from its initial reaction to my presence, though I could still hear the hum of restless voices.

"What brings you to Scotland, my dear?" the lieutenant asked. I didn't warm to his term of endearment. It sounded sincere and patronizing, especially from a young man. I would have much preferred to be called "my dear" by a rosy-cheeked little old lady into whose arms I could pour myself as she murmured words of comfort and security.

"Photography," I said. "I'm shooting pictures for a calendar."

The lieutenant turned to the sergeant, with eyebrows raised in an expression of inquiry.

Stupid answer, I thought.

"Art," I amended. "I'm an artist, landscapes."

"Ah! A painter! Well, that certainly explains the eccentricity of your attire."

I looked down at my long-sleeved shirt and jeans.

"Yes."

I caught the bearded man's eye again. He tilted his head farther, as if he studied me. Clearly, he could hear our conversation. Jet-black eyes now watched me carefully.

"I must say, my dear, that although you are probably permitted a certain license for being an artist, your costume is causing quite a stir. As perhaps is the style of your auburn hair, such that you allow it to hang down your back."

Bemused, I reached up to my ponytail and twirled it around my fingers. Then something snapped.

"I think I should go now," I said abruptly. I started to rise, but with one look from the lieutenant, the sergeant pushed me back down to my seat. His touch was gentle but firm. I wasn't going anywhere.

"No, my dear," Lieutenant Dunston said with a slow shake of his head. "I do not think you should simply run off into the night. What is your name?"

"Lily Brown," I mumbled. Without knowing why, I threw a pleading look in the dark-bearded man's direction.

"Lily? An unusual name to be sure, Miss Brown. I am Lieutenant Solomon Dunston, and this is Sergeant Wilson. We are on the point of returning to Fort William after an arduous week of searching for rebels, but Sergeant Wilson convinced me that we should rest here for the night."

I said nothing.

"And are you staying nearby, Miss Brown? Surely you are not staying here at the Blackbriar Inn, not from the landlady's reception of you."

"No, I'm not. I'm staying with—" I looked over the lieutenant's shoulder again toward the dark-haired man. *Staying with whom?*

"I'm renting a cottage while I paint," I blurted out.

"Surely not alone!" the lieutenant said faintly.

"Yes, alone. I'm very independent," I added.

"Quite!"

The landlady, no longer merely a waitress, arrived with two heaping plates of food, which she set in front of the soldiers.

"We've sent some food out to the stables for yer men," she said, favoring me with another stink eye.

My mouth watered at the hunks of dark-brown bread on the plates. I was hungry.

"Perhaps a plate for the young woman?" the sergeant suggested, apparently catching my expression.

"Nay, Sergeant, I willna serve the likes of her." The landlady shook her head.

"Yes, I think you must," the lieutenant said softly but firmly.

The landlady locked eyes with the lieutenant, lost the stare down, and turned away in a flounce of hips and skirts.

"Oh, thank you," I said. "I *am* hungry."

"How did you come to be outside the inn tonight, miss? It is not proper for a single lady to travel the countryside alone at night." The sergeant was rapidly becoming quite the fatherly figure—full of authority, admonitions and lectures.

I wanted to say I was on my home from granny's, but my predicament didn't really fit the fairy tale.

"I was..." I licked my lips, my eyes darting around the room for inspiration. They landed on the dark-haired man again.

"I was just stopping by to look for my landlord, and there he is!"

I jumped up and dashed around the table, flinging myself onto the bench next to the dark-haired man. He half rose as if to take off, but I grabbed his arm, clinging to the thick material of his black coat.

"Help me," I whispered. "Please help me." I turned a big grin on the surprised stranger.

"Here you are! My roof is leaking!" I said loudly. "When can you fix it?"

Black eyes blinked, and he threw a hasty look toward the lieutenant, who had rotated on his bench to watch me.

"Och, lass, what have ye done?" he growled under his breath. He rose, pulling me up with him. The top of my head came to the middle of his chest.

"Let us go see to yer roof," he mumbled in a deep baritone. He took my arm in his and none too gently guided me around the table toward the door.

"Just a minute!" the lieutenant called out, his quiet voice eerily carrying through the noise of the pub.

My reluctant rescuer froze and rotated slowly, turning me with him. The lieutenant beckoned with one finger, and we moved toward him.

"It is not raining tonight, my good man. Surely you do not intend on working on the roof tonight, do you?"

Lieutenant Dunston was no fool. His face showed nothing more than mild curiosity, but his blue eyes hardened.

"A storm is rolling in, sir. My missus told me so. She kens such things."

I shot a glance up at my companion. His missus? Somehow, the knowledge that he was married bothered me. It shouldn't have. He was helping me out. I looked forward to meeting his missus. Maybe she cooked. Because if all went well, my "landlord" and I were leaving before the landlady brought back my plate of food. I couldn't stay around to ask for a to-go bag.

Lieutenant Dunston eyed my rescuer, studying him from his gray tam to the muddied boots covering the lower half of his charcoal-gray trousers.

"Your wife predicts weather?" he asked with a skeptical smile.

"Aye, that she does."

"Miss Brown called you her landlord. You are not a laird? I would know if you were a laird in this region."

"Nay, Lieutenant. Miss Brown misspoke. I am nowt but a tenant farmer. She is renting a small cottage on my leased land."

The lieutenant nodded. "Yes, of course. She is from America, after all."

"Aye."

"Well, Miss Brown, it seems you are to accompany your 'landlord' to your home. Please take care in the future when venturing out in such unconventional garb and at such a late hour, especially unaccompanied. It is not something that is normally done by ladies of good reputation. I will allow that you are probably unfamiliar with our British customs."

My face flamed upon hearing some of the ribald comments of the men in the room as they stared at us.

"My missus will see to the lass," the stranger said.

"Yes, that would be wise. And your name is…"

My rescuer lifted a finger to his tam.

"Calum Campbell."

"Campbell," the lieutenant repeated softly. "Yes, there are many of you Campbells about here."

"Aye," Calum said.

"Good night then, Miss Brown. Perhaps we shall see you again. Good night, Mr. Campbell."

"Night," Calum said. He tightened his hold on my arm and practically hauled me from the pub. Once outside, he didn't stop to question me as I had expected him to but continued to manhandle me back the way I had come.

"Hey!" I said as we left the lights of the inn and returned to the trail. Fortunately, Calum seemed to know his way as he walked with assurance, even in the dark. "You can stop pulling me now."

I tried to wrench my arm from his grasp, but he held on to me.

"Ye wanted my help, lass. Well, now ye have it!" The timber of his voice suggested not solicitous support, but anger. He pulled me along down the road, and my anxiety mounted to an entirely new level. What had I gotten myself into? I'd run to the first stranger I could find to rescue me from what? The authorities? This dark-haired angry man was much more likely to harm me than was a pale, languid English officer.

"Wait a minute!" I said hoarsely. "I really appreciate your help, I do! But I can take care of myself now."

Of course I couldn't, but he didn't need to know that.

"I dinna ken that ye can, Miss Brown, if that be yer name." He loosened his grip on my arm but did not let go. "Where do ye wish me to escort ye? I canna in good faith leave ye to wander the Highlands at night."

"No, I really am staying in a cottage, just not on your land."

"Nay, lass. No one like ye is renting a cottage hereabouts. I would have heard of such. Everyone would have heard of such."

"Okay, you've got me. I'm not! Can we just go see your missus? Do you have a phone?"

Of course he didn't have a phone. I wasn't in the twenty-first century anymore. I wasn't quite sure why I kept asking that ridiculous question.

"Nay, I dinna have a fone. I dinna ken what such is. Nor do I have a wife."

I stopped short, and rather than wrench my arm out of its socket, he stopped with me.

"No wife?" I tried not to be pleased. I wasn't. In fact, that information frightened me even more. "Then where are you taking me?"

"Well, I have been asking ye where ye wanted to go, but since ye clearly have no idea where ye are, I am taking ye to my cottage. It will no be an easy walk for ye, but I dinna ken what else to do with ye."

"Oh!" His response sounded practical, as if he had no sinister plans to harm me.

"Well, okay," I said slowly. "I did ask you for help. I'll be honest. I'm lost, and I don't know how to get back home at the moment. I'm hungry and I'm tired."

I remembered thinking that his missus would whip up something for me to eat. That hope was dashed.

"Ye can stay the night at my cottage. I didna get a chance to get my food either afore ye accosted me, so I will cook something for our supper."

He took me by the arm again, this time much more gently, and he led me back down the road away from the village. His legs were long, his stride fast, and I had all I could do to keep up with him. Without extra oxygen for conversation, I fell silent, focusing on keeping my balance and his pace.

Calum seemed disinclined to ask me any questions or offer any more information about himself, so we moved in silence. At some point, we turned away from the main road and followed a smaller trail, gaining elevation as we walked. I was disoriented in the dark, having no idea where we were headed.

"It grows steep now, lass. Have a care with yer footing. Ye are fortunate that ye are not hampered by skirts."

"Well, that explains why you don't have a wife," I said breathlessly, still trying to keep up with him, and now taxed by a sharp ascent. "She couldn't possibly get up and down this hill if she did wear skirts."

To my surprise, he chuckled, a warm, resonant laugh that brought a delighted shiver to my spine.

"Aye, that must be the reason I am no married."

The moon peeped out, and I saw that the trail now led through trees.

"Do you live on top of a mountain or something?"

"It seems so," he said. "My cottage lies in the woods. I dinna get many visitors up here, save for the English when they scour the hills looking for Jacobites."

He spat the word "English," and I deduced that he was no fan. I had suspected as much when he interacted with Lieutenant Dunston. I knew the Scottish people had a long history of anger with the English, and I wondered again where I was...or more like "when" I was. What era had I inadvertently fallen into?

"What year is it?"

"I heard ye ask that at the inn, lass. Do ye ken how daft that question seems?"

"Yes. But I still want to hear you tell me."

"1747."

My knees buckled, and something happened to my breathing, as in...I didn't. I sagged against Calum, and he caught me in his arms. For the second time that day, I fainted.

CHAPTER THREE

"Miss Brown! Miss Brown! Lass, are ye ill?"

I awakened to the feel of Calum's roughened hand patting my cheek. He cradled me in his lap. I grabbed his hand and held on to it, mostly to keep him from tapping on my cheek.

"The eighteenth century?" I asked hoarsely.

"What? Och, the year! Aye, the eighteenth century. Are ye ill? Ye fainted."

"Yes, I'm sure I did," I said. Moonlight filtered through the trees, highlighting Calum's face. He peered at me closely, his eyes showing concern—eighteenth-century concern from an eighteenth-century face, the face of an eighteenth-century Highlander. At least, from the hill we were climbing, I assumed I was still in the Highlands. But in the eighteenth century.

I could not stop repeating those words.

"Has Culloden come and gone?"

Calum stiffened and pulled his hand from mine.

"What?"

"Culloden. When was that?"

"1746. Why do ye ask?"

For some reason, I felt him pull away. He didn't exactly throw me off his lap, but he definitely distanced himself from me. Was Culloden something one didn't talk about? What did I know? I was no history buff. I photographed landscapes, not historical markers. If a castle happened to fall into the picture of a misty glen, so much the better, but I didn't care whose castle it was, who had owned it or what battles had been fought in, around and because of it.

I had done a calendar of Ireland's scenic vistas last year, England the year before. This year was meant to be Scotland, Scotland in the twenty-first century.

How had this happened? Why had this happened? And more importantly, how could I make this unhappen?

"No reason," I finally responded. "I just didn't remember my history." I snapped my lips together.

"Aye, I suppose one might call it history, but the Battle at Culloden is still very near and dear to the Highlanders' hearts. The English may have won, but the battle for Scotland will never end."

With that emphatic statement, Calum rose, pulling me to my feet at the same time. He dropped his hands to his sides, and I wobbled, my knees still shaky. I steadied myself by bracing my hands on his wide chest.

"Sorry. I feel a little lightheaded," I said.

"Aye, of course. Forgive me. Can ye travel further? We canna spend the night here."

"Yes."

Calum slipped an arm around my waist and half carried me the rest of the way up the hill. Just when I thought we must have been climbing the Alps, we crested the hill. The moon, fully in its element in a break in the clouds and the absence of trees, shone down on a meadow that stretched out to show even more black hills in the distance.

"I feel like I should start yodeling," I said rather foolishly. "Do you really live up here?"

"Aye, my cottage is no much further."

I heard the distant sound of bleating.

"Sheep?"

"Aye," Calum said.

"Are you a sheepherder?"

"No, not I," he said. "The herder lives some miles away over the hills."

We followed the trail through the meadow into a valley flanked by hills. At some point, we turned sharply away from the meadow and headed into a thick mass of darkness that I recognized as woods by the sound of the leaves in the trees. After about ten minutes, a small stone cottage came into view, and I guessed without entering that this was a one-bedroom deal, if that.

I eyed Calum uneasily. Not only was there no missus, I didn't think there would be a guest bedroom with a lock on the door.

I shivered uncontrollably. The temperature, already cool given that it was September, had dropped even further as we gained elevation. Calum no longer held me around the waist as he had on the ascent, and now that we were no longer expending energy in climbing, the chill set in.

"Ye're freezing, lass," he said, slipping out of his greatcoat and laying it over my shoulders. I snuggled into its warmth. "Come inside. I will get a fire started to warm ye."

One bedroom or one and a spare, I stopped caring as my teeth chattered.

"Yes, a fire," I said.

Calum guided me toward the cottage. Lifting a latch on a small wooden door, he bent to enter and took my hand to pull me in behind him.

"Stay put, and dinna move until I light a candle. I dinna wish ye to harm yerself in the dark."

I pulled his coat tighter around me and waited, noting a small sliver of moonlight coming in through a single window. A yellow glow caught my eye, and I turned to see Calum standing over an oil lantern centered on a small square oak table in the middle of the room.

He gave me a faint smile before striding over to kneel by a stone hearth.

"Please, sit," he said with a look over his shoulder. "I will just set a fire." He nodded toward the table.

I pulled out a worn wooden high-back chair and sat down, keeping his coat around my shoulders. The lamp revealed that the situation was worse than I had feared—there was no bedroom at all. A lone sagging mattress hugged one corner of the room. I couldn't imagine how the sleeping arrangements were going to work out.

"Ye said ye were hungry," Calum said, stacking wood and tinder. "I can make up a stew. I have some oatcakes set by."

"Oh! No bother," I said. "I can just eat oatcakes."

"Nonsense. Ye canna live on oatcakes alone. I will make the stew. It will no take long. I have everything set by. You will remember that I am hungry too."

"What do you do up here all day long?" I asked. "Do you farm? Or…" I couldn't actually think of another option.

The fire took hold in the hearth, and Calum stood, wiping his hands on his trousers. Shed of his coat, I noted he wore a white linen shirt. He loosed the knots of his neckcloth.

"Do?" he said, leaning down to pick up a heavy iron pot, which he hooked on to an iron frame over the fire. "Och, there is plenty to do up here," he said. "I grow a few things, but I dinna farm the land, if that is what ye mean. It is much too high up here to grow proper crops. And I dinna tend to sheep."

From an old battered wooden sideboard, he picked up an earthenware jug of what I assumed was water and poured it into the pot before retrieving some vegetables from a shelf on the wall—some I recognized, some I didn't. He cut the food up and dumped it into the pot.

"Will ye have some ale?"

I watched him in bemusement, trying to keep my eyes on the "kitchen" activities and away from the "bedroom."

"Yes, please," I said in a faint, desperate note. Could I even drink the water here? It wasn't purified. I was sure he just acquired it from some nearby stream. A thought struck me, and I surveyed the one-room cabin again. For that matter, where was the bathroom?

"Where is the..." I didn't have to use it, but I really, really wanted to know where it was.

Calum, pouring ale into two pewter tankards, turned around to look at me.

"Where is what?"

I waggled my eyebrows, as if he could guess. He wasn't guessing though.

"The bathroom."

"Bathroom?" he echoed, setting a tankard down in front of me as he pulled out the chair across the small table and sat down. "Do ye mean a room in which to bathe?"

I shook my head. Well, yes, actually that would be good too, at some point, depending on how long I was stuck there.

"No, where one goes to the bathroom. You know, toilet?"

The corners of Calum's lips curved into a smile.

"Ah! Ye mean the necessary, a privy."

"Yes, that's it." I nodded. I was prepared for an outhouse.

"I have none such. Ye must make do in the woods, as I do."

"What?" I hadn't needed to use the bathroom when I first asked. Now, it felt urgent.

"Aye, do ye wish to attend to matters now? I can take ye to a likely spot."

"Well, actually..."

Calum rose.

"Come then," he said, picking up the lantern. He pulled open the door, and I followed him outside, still clutching his coat. He rounded the corner of the cottage and led me on a small worn trail into a wooded area not more than a few minutes from the house. He handed me the lantern and pulled his coat from my shoulders.

"Ye will no be able to manage the coat, lantern and your clothes. Walk on for a minute or so. I will await ye here."

"Oh, gosh, this is just like camping. I don't suppose you have a tissue?"

"A tissue?" he repeated with a tilt of his head.

"No, don't worry about it. I'll figure it out."

I took the lantern from him and moved away, but not too far. I set the lantern down and retreated behind a shrub of some sort. As many women had done before me, I did my business, drip dried, jumped up and zipped up my jeans before grabbing the lantern and returning to his side.

Calum settled his coat over my shoulders again, and we turned to walk back toward the cottage.

"So what do you do if you have to..."

"Does everyone have a privy in the colonies then, Miss Brown? Ye seem decidedly ignorant in these matters. At the moment, I do wish I had a wife to instruct ye."

At the moment, so did I, contrary to the disappointment I'd experienced when he first mentioned a wife. There were things Calum just wasn't going to be able to help me with. Forget the bathroom! How was I supposed to return to the future?

"I really couldn't say, Mr. Campbell. And yes, I think I am decidedly ignorant in these matters. You're right about that."

We reached the front door, and he pushed it open, allowing me to precede him. The fire had warmed the cottage nicely, and I shrugged out of Calum's coat as I resumed my seat. He took it from me and hung it on a hook by the door.

He moved over to the pot to peer into it before giving it a stir.

"Soon," he said, turning to take his seat once again.

I picked up my ale and took a sip. Warm, stout and yet creamy, it tasted like no beer I'd ever had.

"This is different," I said, assuaging my hunger with a few delicious gulps.

"Is it?" he asked. "From your beers in the Colonies? How so?"

I peered into the mug.

"Well, it looks very dark, but it tastes almost creamy."

"Aye, it's the oats."

I nodded. Sure. Oats. Scotland. Why not?

The liquid warmed my stomach.

"Do ye come from a wealthy family then, Miss Brown? I ask, ye ken, because ye seem..." He paused as if searching for words.

"Decidedly ignorant?" I repeated with a smirk. I swallowed still more of the lovely beer.

"Perhaps I could have worded that more kindly."

"Oh, no. That's fine. Let's see. Do I come from a wealthy family? No, but I have money. I make a pretty good living as a photographer."

"I heard ye use that term at the inn. Ye said ye were a painter?"

"Oh, yes, painter. That's it. Yes, I make pretty good money painting, so I have a bathroom in my house, a privy, a toilet."

My smirk widened to a lopsided grin. "That sounded stupid. As if artists have bathrooms."

Calum watched me with widening eyes.

"Are ye well, Miss Brown?"

"Oh, sure, very well, thank you. How's that stew coming along?"

I definitely needed to eat. The beer had gone right to my head.

"Do you have any more of that ale?" Apparently, I didn't care that the ale was going right to my head.

"Aye," he said, taking my mug over to the sideboard and refilling it. "I think the stew will be ready soon." He set my ale in front of me and busied himself putting oatcakes on a dish, which he also set in front of me.

"Perhaps ye should eat something while we wait."

I snagged an oatcake and bit into it, enjoying the slightly salty taste, which went very well with my beer.

"Oh, that's delicious. Much better than modern oatcakes. Do you make these here or buy them somewhere?"

Calum again tilted his head, as if studying me.

"Modern oatcakes?" he repeated.

I heard my mistake, but the ale allowed me to blithely ignore it.

"I make my own oatcakes. I have plenty of time for such."

"Awesome!" I crunched some more.

"I dinna think they are that good, though I do fancy them myself. What did ye mean by modern oatcakes?"

"Did I say modern?" I shook my head, barely aware that my mouth was still curved into a foolish grin. "I can't imagine why."

"No?" he asked. His *no* must have held a million *o*'s. I loved it!

"Nooooo," I imitated.

Calum's eyes crinkled with his smile.

"Are ye mocking my English then?"

"Noooooo," I said with a laugh. "I think it's charming. I love your accent."

Calum blinked. I wasn't sure, but I thought his cheeks bronzed. It was hard to tell with his beard...and the fire-tinged lighting...and the ale.

"It is a very interesting form of English that ye speak yourself," he said. "I have never met anyone from the Colonies."

"Thank you," I said. "In the United—" I paused. "In America, I don't really have an accent. It's sort of generic."

"Do ye speak any other languages?" he asked.

I shook my head. "No. I did two years of Spanish in high school, but I don't remember much about them."

"Spanish? I dinna ken this 'high school.'"

No, I was sure he didn't. I wasn't about to enlighten him either. At least I hoped I wasn't.

"Do you speak any other languages?" I asked, taking a swig of my ale.

"English," he said with a lift of his lips. "That is my other language."

"Oh, of course," I said with a foolish giggle. "You speak Gaelic, don't you?"

"Aye, Scottish Gaelic."

"Ooooh, say something in Gaelic!" I was rapidly becoming infatuated with the handsome Highlander with the delightful accent. His tall, broad-shouldered figure, lustrous black eyes and the dark wavy hair hugging his shoulders didn't hurt either.

Calum grinned with a shake of his head and rose to check on the stew.

"It is forbidden to speak Gaelic. Dinna ye ken that?"

"No, I didn't! Why?"

Calum dished stew onto some pewter plates and brought them to the table, along with spoons.

I dug in, burning my tongue in the process.

"Take care." He laughed. "It is hot!"

"Yes, I can see that." I healed my sore tongue with another gulp of ale.

"So why can't you speak Gaelic?" I repeated.

"Och! I do, of course. I dinna care what the English have to say, but I dinna speak it in public. The English think that by banning the wearing of kilts, the speaking of Gaelic and confiscating our weapons, they can prevent another rebellion. They will not succeed, of course. Scotland will have her freedom!"

Even in my drunken haze, I thought I remembered that Culloden was the last rebellion for Scotland.

"Wait! Culloden came and went last year, right? Didn't someone say that?" I blew on my spoonful of stew.

"Aye, the battle was fought in April last year."

"Well, I hate to tell you this, Calum, but I'm pretty sure Scotland's rebellions against the English are over."

The man who had rescued me from a hairy situation, who had half carried me up the mountain to his home, had given me his coat, had cooked for me and whom I'd come to trust, jumped up from his seat and banged his palm flat on the table.

"How dare ye!" he shouted, leaning into me. "How dare ye speak so flippantly of what ye dinna ken!"

I cowered in my chair, my eyes wide. As if Calum's outburst shocked him more than it had shocked me—which was significant—he strode toward the door, grabbed his coat and stormed out.

Chapter Four

I stared at the door swinging open. A small part of my brain wondered that it hadn't closed when Calum slammed it, until I noted that the wooden latch hadn't fallen into place.

I realized I'd been holding my breath, and I tried to inhale, but a painful tightness in my chest prevented it. I rose to walk to the doorway, startled to find my knees shaking. In fact, my entire body trembled.

I wasn't used to being yelled at, certainly not by strange men, but I didn't think that was the cause of my reaction. As I stared out into the darkness, I realized that my body was probably reacting to the entirety of my experiences over the past few hours, to the fact that somehow I had traveled through time and had no idea how to get back.

Here I was, stuck in the eighteenth century—without a bathroom, without a cell phone, without a passport—and I didn't know what to do. Who could I tell? Who could help me? And where on earth was the river, the location where I'd apparently traveled through time?

Calum's flare of anger had scared me, I couldn't lie, and I trusted him a whole lot less than I had a few moments ago, lulled by the tasty ale and the hot stew.

Gone was my idea that Calum was a kind, sweet, nurturing gentleman. Oh no! His dark looks had suggested an uncompromising, rugged man, but one really didn't expect a man's looks to match his personality. I mean, one did actually, but surely that was a generalization. Wasn't it? Blond men were naturally sweet and kind, redheads full of fun, dark-haired men brooding? No.

What did I know? I was twenty-five, and I'd had exactly one boyfriend in my life—a fiancé really, until he broke it off the year before because he'd met someone more compatible, a high school senior whose photographs he'd taken in our studio. We'd been together throughout most of high school and college, but that was then. He'd been a blond—sweet and kind. Now, he was sweet and kind with someone else.

I turned from the painful thoughts of Shane and stepped outside. The moon lit my surroundings like a silver streetlight, and I scanned the woods for signs of Calum. I wasn't sure if I wanted him to come back, but I knew I definitely didn't want him *not* to return.

What I wanted most of all was for the sun to come up. It felt like I'd been in the eighteenth century for about a century, though I was sure it had only been a few hours. But my time here had all been in darkness. Surely things would look better when the sun came up, wouldn't they?

The cool night air did nothing to lessen my shivering, so I returned to the warmth of the cottage, dropping the latch on the door. I seated myself back down at the table and finished off my cup of ale. My shivering stopped, though I'd lost my appetite. I stared into the fire while I waited for Calum to return. Eventually, my head started nodding, and I almost fell out of my chair on one occasion.

I eyed the bed in the corner and then the door. Was Calum coming back tonight at all? Surely he wasn't leaving me here on my own, was he?

With heavy eyelids, I rose and made my way to the bed with the thought that if I could just rest for a few minutes, I'd be fine. I think I needed to sleep off the effects of the ale more than anything.

I didn't hear Calum return, but when I opened my eyes the next morning, sunlight filtered in through the window, and Calum lay on a gray blanket on the floor in front of the hearth. The fire was dead, and my breath came out in a fog. Clearly, it was quite frosty in the higher elevations of the Highlands in September.

A length of tartan cloth lay across me, and I realized Calum had covered me up. I propped myself up on one elbow and studied him.

The soft sunlight highlighted his face. In repose, he looked more relaxed, less forbidding, less troubled. I hadn't realized that his face had carried such an unsettled expression before now, with the exception of when I'd thrown myself at his mercy in the pub. That had clearly panicked him. He looked far younger than I had originally thought, maybe around thirty. His beard made it hard to gauge his age.

As if Calum felt me watching him, his eyes opened with an alertness unusual for one who had just woken up. He jumped up and grabbed his blanket from the floor to fold it before placing it on the foot of the bed.

"Forgive me," he said without looking at me. He busied himself with rebuilding the fire and lighting it. "I should no have stormed out as I did. It was wrong of me."

I sat up and slipped my feet onto the floor, noting I hadn't even removed my shoes before falling asleep…or passing out. The table had been cleared, and I assumed he must have done that while I slept.

"Where did you go?"

"To the woods," he said. "I was no gone long, but ye were asleep afore I returned."

I stood, feeling the need to visit the woods myself. I folded the tartan blanket and set it on the bed.

"I'm sorry I seemed insensitive last night. I'm very sorry." I wasn't about to bring up the rebellion against England again. He wasn't wrong. I had been flippant with a subject about which I knew little and, frankly, was affected by even less. I was American with a smattering of Scottish ancestry as well as Irish and English. But I had no particular Celtic calling, no family who had celebrated their Anglo-Saxon heritage, no kilt hanging in my closet or secret desire to play the bagpipes.

I had chosen to do a pictorial calendar of Scotland only because all things Scottish were in vogue at the moment. I had no idea why I had traveled in time, but it had nothing to do with some mystical identification with the Highlands. I was too practical to imagine any such thing.

For me, the rebellion of the Scottish Highlanders against England was a historical fact. To Calum, in 1747, it was apparently still a painful reality. I wondered whether he had fought at Culloden. Hadn't most of the Highlanders in the battle been slaughtered?

I wanted to ask, but in the interest of keeping the peace, I held my tongue.

Calum shook his head. "Nay, no matter what the subject, I bullied ye shamefully, and I am truly sorry."

His *r*'s rolled from his tongue in a sensuous way that made my heart race. I may not have had any Celtic yearnings, but I sure did love a Scottish accent.

"Are ye hungry?" he asked, finally turning to look at me. More *r*'s. My face flamed as I nodded, hoping he didn't notice how enthralled I was with his speech.

"Good," he said. "I will have some porridge ready in a minute. Sit down and have some ale."

I eyed the tankard of ale on the table.

"Oh, no! I don't think I can drink more ale. I'm not really used to drinking that much, and certainly not for breakfast."

Calum, stirring a pot over the fire, looked over his shoulder again.

"What do ye drink in the Colonies then?"

"Water? Coffee? Tea?"

"I think I have some tea in a tin somewhere," he said, leaving the hearth to rummage in a cupboard of the sideboard. "Aye, here it is. I can set some water aside to boil for yer tea."

"Thank you," I said gratefully. I'd soon become a raging alcoholic if I spent too much time in eighteenth-century Scotland.

"So, I was wondering..." I began. "I know I've asked you this before, but I'm not sure you really answered me. How do you make a living up here?"

"A living?" Calum repeated, keeping his attention on the porridge.

I had the distinct feeling that he was prevaricating. I should know. I used the same tactics.

"A living?" I repeated in question form. "For instance, how do you buy your porridge? The vegetables for the stew? The ale?"

Calum stretched his neck from side to side, as if it ached, and then he turned and picked up some plates to set on the table.

"Is it a custom in the Colonies to ask people where they get their money? It is no what we do here in Scotland."

He smiled as if to soften his words, but the smile did not reach his eyes.

I gulped. Calum was inconsistent, to say the least. I had no idea how he would react to comments, and frankly, I didn't trust him. Although Shane had ultimately been unfaithful to me, during the majority of our years together, he had been completely predictable—always pleasant, always kind, always transparent—even at the end when he told me he had fallen in love with another woman.

I was struggling with Calum at the moment. I couldn't predict his reactions. He seemed closed off at times and open at others. In fact, he seemed to have more secrets than I did.

If there had been a fleeting moment when I wanted to tell him that I'd traveled through time, that I was lost in time, that urge had passed. I simply didn't trust how he would react to the news. I didn't trust him.

"No, of course not. It's not a custom. I was just being rude." I affected a cheesy grin, not feeling at all like grinning. I began to wonder about returning to the village, but I couldn't say that I trusted anyone there either. And I worried about the soldiers. Even if they had moved on to Fort William by now, it was likely that someone would call them if I revealed—or they discovered—that I had traveled through time.

I looked down at my jeans. That was a problem. No, I couldn't return to the village.

"I don't suppose you have a spare skirt laying around somewhere, do you? From the missus that isn't here? You know, just in case I need to run into the village?"

Calum paused in the act of spooning porridge onto my plate.

"I dinna have any women's garments up here, but I can return to the village and find something for ye." He sat down across from me.

"Why do ye dress in men's clothing? I dinna ken much about the Colonies, but surely it is verra unusual for women to wear trews?"

"Trews?" I stalled. The word sounded enough like trousers that I guessed its meaning.

"Aye, trews, such as I wear now."

I picked up my spoon and ladled in some way-too-hot porridge, burning my mouth but keeping a smile on my face. Calum set a small, surprisingly delicate porcelain teacup and saucer in front of me and poured some tea into it. The rose-patterned set seemed inconsistent with the stark amenities of the modest cabin.

"Don't Scots wear kilts?" I asked as another stalling tactic. Now that I asked the question, I wondered. No one in the pub had worn a kilt either that I could tell. In fact, no sort of tartan or plaid. Other than the cloth Calum had covered me with, I saw no patterned garments.

"Ye may have forgotten that I mentioned the wearing of kilts has been forbidden by the English."

"Oh, I did! I'm sorry." I *had* forgotten some of his words, so aghast had I been at his rage.

Calum shrugged, the gesture more bitter than resigned. "It is a disgraceful attempt to turn us into Englishmen. They can try to take away our kilts, our language, our swords, but they can never change who we are."

He dug into his porridge, and I watched him covertly, more curious than ever about whether he had fought at Culloden.

These are the things I knew about Calum Campbell: he was secretive, he had an unknown source of income, he was a Scottish patriot, he was a troubled, angry man, and he couldn't leave females in distress, even if he wanted to. I wasn't sure what all that amounted to, but that was what I knew.

"Do you have family?" Oh, and he was unmarried! He had no missus. If he was telling the truth about that.

He eyed me narrowly. I thought maybe he wasn't going to respond. I hoped he wasn't going to jump down my throat again. I had a bunch more questions!

"My parents passed. I had no brothers or sisters. And you? Do you have family in the Colonies?"

I shook my head.

"No, both my parents died a few years ago in an accident."

"Och, my condolences," he said with a shake of his head. "An accident?"

I wasn't about to explain cars, wet highways and semitrucks, so I nodded. "Yes, an accident. How did your parents pass away?"

Calum hesitated for a moment, and his face darkened. He finally responded.

"The flux," he said. "My parents traveled to Glasgow and were felled by the disease there."

"I'm so sorry," I said. "Do you mean the 'flu,' like a cold, only worse?"

"I have heard it called dysentery," Calum said. "It is not uncommon in the cities. They thought to enjoy themselves for a wee spell in the city, but that was not meant to be."

Dysentery! I looked down at my half-eaten porridge and set down my spoon.

"Dinna fear the disease up here," Calum said. "It is no common in the Highlands."

I nodded. So he said!

I rose, the call of nature, which I'd forgotten, now pressing.

"I'm going to…" I nodded toward the door.

"Aye, of course," Calum said, rising.

"Oh no! I'm good. I can find my way."

Calum eyed me, almost suspiciously. I couldn't hold back.

"Wait! Do you think I'm going to run away? Even if I did, Mr. Campbell, that would be my business, right? I'm not your prisoner, am I?"

I really didn't want the answer to that question, unless it was an emphatic no.

As I spoke, I had moved to the door and lifted the latch.

"Nay, of course ye are no my prisoner!" he snapped. "Ye may remember that I didna choose to come to yer aid but was forced into it when ye catapulted yerself into my arms."

"Catapulted?" I repeated. He wasn't wrong. "Okay, yes, well, I did ask for your help. That's right. I just need you to know that all I want from you is your help. I don't want anything else, got it? I don't want to be your prisoner, I don't want to spend the rest of my life up here, and I don't want anything else from you. If you need a missus, you'll have to get her some other way."

Calum's jaw dropped, as well it should have. What a rant! And an ungrateful one at that. I'd become a stranger to myself.

"I'm sorry," I said immediately. "I'm sorry. I think I'll just go to the bathroom now."

I turned and hurried out the door, a small part of my mind concerning myself with what I was supposed to do in the absence of toilet tissue.

Ten minutes and two leaves later, I reassembled my clothing and strolled back through the woods to the cabin. Sunlight peeped through the tall trees, and I wished that I had my camera. It had not traveled through time with me, and I supposed it lay on the riverbank where I'd set down my bag. Two weeks' worth of work now lost and a thousand dollars in camera equipment. I didn't suppose my bag would still be there when I returned. If I returned.

The flattened trunk of a felled tree caught my eye, and reluctant to return to the cabin without my game face on, I sat down to ponder my dilemma.

The only thing I could think of was to return to the same place in the river where I'd fainted and try to figure out how I'd traveled in time. I had splashed water on my face—cold, tingling water that had somehow made me dizzy. And then I had fainted.

I wasn't sure how to find that spot again. It had to be along the road to the village, because I'd first seen the soldiers and then followed them without turning off. But I had no idea where I was now. Calum had led me up into the hills in the dark, and even if I found the path leading back down to the valley below, I wasn't sure I could find my way back to the river...or even the village.

"Miss Brown?" I heard Calum call. Through the trees, I saw him approaching. He had changed out of his trews, as he called them, and now sported a beautiful length of blue tartan around his legs—a kilt. The kilt swayed gracefully against his muscular legs. It wasn't the typical kilt I'd seen in the twenty-first century, but was full and long, hanging well below his knees in the back.

"Here," I called out.

He approached, and I noted that his hair was wet and slicked back, as if he'd washed it.

"You had a bath," I said in a bemused tone. Handsome was simply too ordinary a word to describe the highlander. He had changed into a clean shirt as well and wore a dark-brown waistcoat that accentuated the narrowness of his waist. I noticed that a length of his kilt was tucked into a broad belt at his waist.

"Aye, I bathed," he said, running long fingers through his thick dark curls. "Did ye wish to bathe? I left some warm water in the bowl."

"A sponge bath?" I asked. Yes, of course. I still hadn't seen anything resembling a bathroom. "Sure, that would be great!"

"I laid out a towel and some soap. I will await ye out here," he said taking my seat on the stump.

I walked back to the cabin and eyed the steaming bowl of water on the table in the middle of the room. The bowl was quite beautiful, porcelain like my teacup, and I wondered how a man who lived in a cabin in the woods came by such delicate objects. True to his word, Calum had left me a soft linen towel and a bar of what smelled like lavender soap. Lavender. Scotland. Of course.

I looked around the room but could find no cubby to hide behind, so I guessed I was to bathe in the middle of the cabin. I peeled off my clothes, washed up, dried off and then re-dressed, wishing that I had fresh clothing. I had no idea how to wash my hair, but it really needed some soap and water…and a shower.

I draped the towel around my shoulders and carried the bowl of water and soap outside. Bending over, I managed to pour half the water onto my head, set down the bowl, rub soap into my hair and rinse it with the rest of the water. I created quite a muddy mess by the entrance, and I hoped Calum wouldn't mind.

Truthfully, the act reminded me of a camping trip I'd taken with my parents. In the absence of a shower, my mother had washed my hair in just such a way, although the water then had been cold. At least Calum had left me warm water.

After towel drying my hair, I returned the bowl to the cabin and made my way back to the woods where Calum now lay prone on the stump, his face upturned to a ray of sunlight filtering in through the trees. He opened his eyes and looked at me, raising himself to a sitting position.

"Yer hair is quite curly," he said, eying me. I had tried to drag my fingers through my hair but hadn't succeeded very well.

"Yes, it is," I said with a smile. "I don't suppose you have a comb?"

"I do," he said, rising. "It is in the cottage. I regret that I dinna have a length of ribbon set by that ye could tie up yer hair."

I ran my fingers through my still-damp hair and shook it. "That's all right. I've got most of the tangles out, and I have a band in my pocket." I reached into my pocket and withdrew it, pulling my hair up and twisting it into a ponytail, not something I normally did when it was wet.

Calum tilted his head and eyed my quizzically.

"While it is true that I have no met anyone from the Colonies, I canna believe our customs are so different. Do the ladies dress their hair so simply, allowing it to fall down their backs?"

I dropped my hands self-consciously. "Ummm…I can't say."

"Ye canna say? I dinna ken yer meaning."

"I can't speak for other women. This is how I wear my hair." My brief answer seemed to surprise him, and he closed his mouth and rose to head for the cabin.

"Calum," I began, following him. I regretted my terse response.

"Aye?"

"I need to return to the river."

Chapter Five

Calum stopped and turned to me.

"To the river? I will admit I have been wondering when ye would tell me where ye wanted to go, where yer cottage truly is, but the river? Do ye mean the one in the valley?"

I nodded.

"I know I've been a bit enigmatic, Calum, and I'm sorry. I can't explain everything. Please trust me when I say that I am lost and that I think I can find my way home if I return to the river."

He stopped outside the cottage door and looked down at me.

"Is yer cottage close to the river then?"

I nodded. "Yes, it is."

"I am no aware of a cottage near the river," he said. "But if ye think ye ken where it is, I will take ye down there. I take it ye wish to go now then? I must don a pair of trews afore we go. I canna be seen wearing my kilt."

I nodded in response to his question, looking down at the fascinating length of material draped around his waist.

"Yes, the forbidden thing. You don't wear that thing every day though, do you?" Although, privately I thought he should. There was something inherently masculine in the garment. It was unexplainable.

"My kilt?" He looked down at the blue plaid cloth. "Och, I wear it often, have done all my life. I am no used to wearing trews. They bind me."

He smiled quickly and popped into the cabin while I waited outside. He returned in five minutes, re-dressed in his trews and carrying his coat.

"Do ye wish to wear this?" he asked.

"Thank you," I said, allowing him to lay it over my shoulders. I slipped my arms into the sleeves, which covered my hands. The morning was cool, though I suspected it might warm up during our journey back down the hills.

"Come then," he said, leading me away from the cabin and through the woods. We emerged into the open meadow I had seen last night. Soft fall grass melted away toward even more hills, looking as if someone had recently run a riding mower across a massive lawn. The craggy rocks of the hills beyond indicated that they rose above the tree line.

We followed the path down the middle of the meadow that looked, from the droppings, as if some sort of farm animal traveled it often. Sheep, I presumed.

I wanted to take the opportunity to find out more about Calum before I tried to make my way back to the twenty-first century. If I never saw him again, I would always wonder about him.

"Why do you live up here, Calum?"

He looked down at me and then returned his gaze to the path ahead.

"I dinna like to be bothered," he said.

"Oh! Well, I must have been a big bother, huh?"

"Nay," he said. "The lieutenant was taking a fair amount of interest in ye. No one likes that, especially if one has secrets."

"You have secrets, Calum."

"Aye, that I do."

"No chance you want to tell me any of them?"

"I think that would not be wise, lass. At least no for me. And ye? What of yer secrets?"

I looked up at him, and I wanted to tell him the truth, but then I shrugged. He could never understand time travel. I came from the future, where life in outer space was possible, and even I couldn't understand time travel. But a small part of my brain pondered the idea of telling him my secret right before I traveled back in time. That was if I *could* travel back in time. If he stood there and watched me, he would surely wonder what had happened to me.

We soon reached the crest of the hill, and we began our descent, a slow journey in which Calum held my arm and supported me down the trail. The descent was much quicker then our ascent the night before, and to my surprise, an unexpectedly poignant form of regret started to well up inside me. If I could reverse whatever had happened to me when I reached the river, then I would travel forward in time to the twenty-first century, leaving eighteenth-century Scotland behind.

I would leaving knowing very little about historic Scotland, though I suspected I would be one of the few, if not the only, living person to have experienced the eighteenth century in real time. Others who might have accidentally traveled back in time would have relished the opportunity to explore a historical past that I could only read about. But in my anxiety to return to the present—to the known and familiar—I rushed headlong back to the river where it all started.

I would never see Calum again. I would never know what happened to him. I would never know his secrets.

We reached the bottom of the trail, and Calum lowered his arm, leaving me to walk at his side. I had enjoyed his strong yet gentle guidance, and I missed his touch.

I gave myself a good mental shake to snap out of it. If it was possible, I was leaving, and I couldn't bring him with me, so it was best I got over my newly discovered infatuation as fast as I could.

"How long until we reached the river?"

"It is no far," he said he said. "We will reach it in under an hour."

"Oh, so soon?"

He looked down at me with that adorable tilt to his head.

"Are ye no ready to go home?"

I should have answered decisively, enthusiastically, and forcefully, but my body took over, and I shrugged, stuffed my hands in my jeans pockets like a child and shuffled along beside him.

"Yes of course, I have to get back."

"Aye, as ye have said. To yer cottage."

He eyed me quizzically.

"Well, let's keep marching." I flashed him a bright smile and turned my face resolutely forward.

I still didn't recognize my surroundings. We hadn't reached the river yet. We followed a trail now flanked by tall grasses, leaving the hills behind.

I thought I would hear the river before I saw it. I had been listening to my surroundings, waiting to hear babbling or rushing or trickling water, but the river came into view before I knew it.

I hesitated, staring at the watery length. What was I supposed to do now?

"We are here," Calum announced unnecessarily.

"So we are."

"Where do ye go from here?"

"From here?" I asked faintly.

"Aye, from here."

"Oh, I'm not sure," I mumbled.

"Lass, please tell me ye ken where yer cottage is. I would no have brought you back to the valley if I suspected ye would declare yerself lost again. Do ye wish to find yerself in the hands of the soldiers again?

It seems to me that ye have many secrets of yer own that they might find interesting."

I made the decision. It was time.

I turned to Calum and tilted my head back to face him squarely.

"I don't have a cottage here in your time."

He reared his head in confusion and opened his mouth to speak, but I hurried on.

"Calum, don't burn me at the stake or anything, but I come from the twenty-first century." My body shook with reaction, but I took a deep breath and continued. "I'm not from here. I'm not visiting. I'm not painting. I don't know why I traveled through time. I was walking on the trail next to the river, taking pictures, and I stopped to test the waters, so to speak. And voila! Here I am. Just that simple. I traveled through time."

Though I'd started my disclosure with confidence, I had soon dropped my gaze from his startled eyes and found myself staring at the dirt road, wider than it was in the twenty-first century. I raised my head to gauge his reaction.

Calum did that head-tilting thing again, and my heart rolled over.

"I know you're confused," I said. "I'm confused too, but probably not as much as you are, except about you. I'm confused about you, but you're probably not as confused about you as I am."

Calum's eyes widened and then narrowed.

"Woman! Desist! What on earth are ye blathering about? I ken ye believe ye have traveled through time, but what are ye going on about with who is more confused than whom?" He shook his head and pivoted away from me, hooking his hands on his hips. He didn't move but appeared to be thinking as he looked up toward the hills and then down at the ground.

I waited, my heart pounding. I wasn't sure what to expect. For all I knew, Calum was about to turn around and haul me off to the local gaol or the English soldiers or a local priest for an exorcism.

No, I couldn't wait.

"Calum?" I asked hesitantly.

His wavy hair bounced across his shoulders as he shook his head. He turned slowly, and I braced myself for the unknown.

"I canna bring myself to believe yer tale, lass, nor do I believe ye are lying. I dinna ken what to believe. Are ye a witch?"

Visions of burning at the stake, a la Salem witch trials, robbed me of breath.

"No!" I almost shrieked. "I don't believe in witches. Most of the people in my country don't believe in witches anymore. Well, not those who have supernatural powers. Well, some might, but sort of a clairvoyance kind of thing. But no! I'm not a witch!"

Calum watched me with seeming fascination.

"Do ye ever give any brief answers, lass?"

"Well, I'm nervous," I said, stuffing my hands into my pockets again and scuffing the ground with the toe of my shoe. "So, yeah, I'm babbling."

"What do ye wish to do? What do ye wish *me* to do?"

I looked up.

"I guess I'm going to try to travel back through time. I don't belong here. I couldn't live here. I stand out too much. I just couldn't make it here."

"I agree that ye do stand out, but that is due to yer clothing. Why do ye think ye canna live here in Scotland?"

"No, not Scotland. I could live in Scotland very easily. It's wonderful here. The eighteenth century. I can't live in the eighteenth century."

His eyes narrowed for a moment before softening. He nodded.

"What did ye do then afore ye believed ye traveled through time? Did ye drink from the river?"

I shook my head. "No, I just splashed some water on my face." I stared at the river. "But I'm not sure this is the place. I think it might have been closer to the village. How far is the village from here?"

"No more than half an hour."

"Oh!" I said, nonplussed. I really had no idea where I was. "Well, I followed the soldiers into town for about a half hour, so maybe this is close enough."

"Close enough?" Calum asked, clearly confused. I couldn't help him. I was confused too.

"Close enough to where I...appeared."

I stepped off the path to move toward the river, and in doing so, I must have startled Calum, because he grabbed my arm.

"Wait!" he growled in a husky voice.

I looked down at his hand on my arm and then up at his troubled face.

"I'm not going to leave without saying good-bye," I said softly.

He released my arm.

I smiled and crossed the road to kneel on the bank of the river. Calum followed me, and to my surprise, he dropped to his knees at my side.

"And ye did naethin more than splash water on yer face? No incantations? No spells?"

"Nope, that was it."

I stared down at the fast-moving water. The darkness suggested that this portion of the river ran deep.

"If this works, I'll probably just disappear, Calum," I murmured. I turned my head toward him. "Thank you for everything. You've been so kind. I'm so glad to have met you."

Calum took my hand in his and pressed it to his lips.

"And I am happy to have met ye, Miss Brown," he said.

My heart melted at the warm touch of his lips on my hand. Calum would be so easy to fall in love with. Maybe I was already halfway there. Strong, competent, intelligent, reliable. Handsome. Did he even have any flaws? Other than his secrets? And his temper?

He released my hand, and I gave him a tremulous smile, hoping with all my heart that I wasn't about to cry. I turned my attention to the water, staring at it, wondering at its power.

"Don't touch me when I splash the water," I whispered. "You don't want to find yourself stuck in the twenty-first century."

"No? Would it be so bad? Ye would be there." Calum's smile took my breath away.

"Yes," I said. At that moment, I wished I could take him with me, but I couldn't even figure out how to splash water on my face and hold his hand at the same time.

"Farewell, lass. Safe journey," Calum said.

"So, you believe me?" I gave him a half smile.

"We shall soon see."

I nodded. There was really nothing left to say.

"Good-bye, Calum."

In one swift movement, I rose up on my knees, bent over and grabbed some cold water to bring to my face.

"Wait!" Calum grabbed my right hand, spilling much of the water cupped in my hands. I must have still had enough water in my left hand, because I saturated my face. But nothing tingled—not my hands, not my face. And I was still in the eighteenth century.

"Calum!" I gasped. "What are you doing?"

He released my hand quickly and sank back on his knees.

"I dinna ken," he said with a confused shake of his head. "I should no have taken hold of ye. Forgive me."

He rose and moved away, turning around to face me.

"Try again, lass. I will no disturb ye again."

I stared at him, an ache forming in my throat. Oh, how I wanted to take him with me.

He laced his hands behind his back and nodded encouragingly.

"Go now," he said softly.

I nodded, ignored the hot tears slipping down my cheeks and bent over to scoop up some water.

"Good-bye, Calum," I whispered as I splashed the water on my face. The chill took my breath away. I kept my eyes closed and waited for the tingling, the swirling dizziness I had experienced before. Nothing.

I opened my eyes, and resisting the urge to look over my shoulder, I scooped up another handful of water and threw it on my face. I pressed my wet hands against my now cold cheeks, keeping my eyes tightly shut as I anticipated something…anything out of the ordinary.

"Lass?" A quiet voice penetrated my concentration.

I sank back to my knees and opened my eyes. The hills of the Highlands rose before me—patches of pale-green and rust-brown grasses fading into gray granite. Several dainty waterfalls trickled down gullies, feeding the river. The sun shone down on my head, surprisingly warm for September.

"Lass, can ye hear me?"

I looked over my shoulder at Calum, now taking a cautious step toward me. I watched in bemusement as he came to my side and knelt down beside me. My thoughts were a jumble of confusion, indecision, excitement, despair, anxiety and joy.

"It didn't work," I said pointlessly. I turned my attention back toward the river and stared down into its dark depths.

"Nay, it seems not," he said. He took one of my hands in his warm grasp. "I hope I didna ruin it for ye."

Comforted by his touch, if not a little breathless, I shook my head.

"No, I doubt it. If it was going to work, it would have, right?"

I looked up at Calum as if he had the answer.

"I canna say, lass. I dinna ken how ye got here in the first place."

"Me either now. I thought it was the water. I bent down, splashed my face with water and woke up in the eighteenth century."

"Is this a common occurrence in yer time? This time travel?"

"We write stories about it, but no one has ever actually done it. So no, I am the first person I know to have ever traveled through time. Odd, don't you think? Why me? I'm not special."

"Perhaps ye were sent here for a reason."

I looked up at Calum, meeting his warm dark eyes. I shrugged helplessly.

"Why?"

Chapter Six

"I dinna ken, lass. What do ye wish to do now?" He continued to hold my hand in his, making it hard for me to think.

"I don't know." I returned my gaze to the river, studying its mysteries.

"We canna stay here, and I must see to some clothing for ye. Ye canna prance about in yer men's trews much longer, no if ye wish to avoid bringing more unwanted notice to yerself...or me."

I thought about his words.

"So, you're hiding?" I asked. "Keeping a low profile? But why did you go into the village, to the pub?"

"I didna think to see the English soldiers come in. I thought that particular patrol had left the area, but I was wrong. I had every intention of slipping out of the pub when ye threw yerself at me."

Calum grinned.

"I did not throw myself at you," I said weakly. Of course I had.

"Aye, ye did. But what's done is done, and I have the charge of ye now, lost as ye are."

My shoulders sagged even farther.

"I'm sorry. I'd like to tell you that I can manage on my own, but I don't think I can."

"Never ye mind that, lass. Women dinna generally manage on their own here in Scotland, unless they are poor widows. Even then, they can seek shelter with their clan."

"Great. A hundred and fifty years before women get the right to vote in the US," I mumbled under my breath.

"What's that, lass?"

"Nothing," I replied. "Thank you, Calum. What do you think I should do now?"

He chewed on his lips for a moment, turning his gaze toward the road.

"I will take ye to the inn. The landlady is fond of me, and she can give us a dress or two for ye. Perhaps she can even find a room for ye."

"The landlady?" I shuddered. "Oh, no! That woman couldn't stand me."

"Och, lass. That was only because ye were a stranger…and dressed as ye are. She will take kindly to ye once she kens ye are a friend of mine."

"Please don't make me stay there, Calum. Can't I say with you? At least until I figure out an alternative?"

Calum tilted his head and studied my face.

"It is no proper, lass." He shook his head gently.

I swallowed hard, already planning my escape from the inn after he dropped me off.

"Okay," I said.

"Okay?"

"I agree."

Calum pulled me to my feet.

"The hour is early, and I may be able to take ye into the inn by the back door. I hope the soldiers have gone."

We followed the trail toward the village, which, as I had thought, was only a half hour away. The journey in the daytime was beautiful, following the river through a valley for a while until the river coursed away.

True to his word, Calum slipped me into the back door of the inn. We entered a busy kitchen, bustling with the landlady and several young girls wearing stained mobcaps over their hair and dingy aprons over drab-gray homespun dresses. No revealing necklines for these teenagers, though none of them looked as if they had enough meat on their bones to fill out a décolletage.

"Calum!" The landlady said, pivoting to stare at us as one of the girls whispered in her ear. "What are ye doing with the likes of her?" She eyed me up and down, as she had last night. I was fairly sure this woman was not going to change her opinion of me just because Calum wanted her to. No, I definitely wasn't planning on staying.

"Now, Mary," Calum said. "Be kind. This is my friend, Miss Brown. She has come from America, and she needs a room and some proper Scottish clothing. I ken ye will help us."

Mary pushed the ogling young cook back toward her work and eyed us narrowly.

"Calum, dinna try to foist a female of her kind upon me. Ye ken I run a reputable inn. I canna have her sort staying here."

"Mary!"

I gasped as Calum's voice took on a thunderous note. His face had darkened, his thick dark brows narrowing above snapping eyes.

"Miss Brown is no such woman, Mary. She is a lady. I will no brook insults to her character. I am willing to pay for her room for as long as she needs."

Mary blinked at the anger in Calum's voice. She looked from me to Calum before shrugging.

"If ye promise me she will keep to herself, I can let her have the wee room in the attic. It isna much but will do for a young woman. Ye are paying?"

Calum, seemingly disgusted with Mary's reaction, nodded.

"And a dress, please."

"I will give her something of mine," she said grudgingly.

"Good. Thank ye. Do ye think we could have some lunch here in yer kitchen? I dinna wish to subject Miss Brown to further scrutiny in the pub."

"Aye, ye can take a meal at the end of the table, and then I will show the young woman to her room. I canna allow ye to accompany her up there, of course."

"Of course," Calum said in a voice dripping with sarcasm.

Mary turned her back, and Calum led me to a rickety, wooden high-back chair in front of a long rectangular oak table. The young cooks did their prep work on the opposite end closest to the hearth.

"Forgive me," Calum said, seating himself and leaning forward to speak in a low voice. "I didna expect such rudeness from a lady who has always treated me with kindness."

"Well, you're a single man, so there's that."

He pursed his lips.

"Ye are suggesting she has only been kind because I am no married?"

"Ummm...yes?" Men! Such dunces!

He frowned. "She seems verra friendly to all her customers, married or no."

"Who are all men."

Calum blinked and chuckled. "Aye, who are all men. Ye are right. I didna notice afore."

"Men never do," I said.

"I fear that yer room will be a wee thing, as an attic room must be, but I hope ye will be comfortable."

"I really don't feel good about you paying for all this." I paused. "But I don't know what else to do, not if you won't let me stay with you." I gave him a hopeful look.

"It is no possible, lass. It is best ye stay here in the village." He shook his head regretfully.

I nodded, determined more than ever to leave the inn as soon as Calum departed. I wasn't sure where I would go, but I wasn't going to stay there.

Mary settled a couple of plates and tankards of ale in front of us, and Calum and I ate. Unclear about what I was eating and somewhat short of a hearty appetite, I picked at my food. The cooks continued to throw curious glances in our direction. Several pairs of eyes lingered on Calum. I knew how they felt. I wanted to gawk at his handsome dark self too, and probably had been.

We finished eating, and Calum rose and crossed the kitchen to talk to Mary. I saw him reach into his coat pocket and withdraw a small bag, from which he extracted some coins to settle into Mary's hand. With a nod, he returned to my side. Mary followed.

I swallowed hard.

"Mary will see ye to yer room now. Stay there. Dinna go out. Dinna walk about alone. Dinna go into the pub to eat. Mary will have one of the girls bring yer meals to ye. And some clothing. Even when ye're properly dressed, dinna go outside alone. It is no safe for a young woman outside on her own. Mary might allow one of the lasses to accompany ye on a walk tomorrow after the noon meal if ye like." He turned to confirm that with the landlady who rolled her eyes and nodded.

"I will return to see ye the day after."

My heart sank.

"Two days?" I whispered, self-consciously aware that Mary watched us.

"Aye! I have some business to attend to tomorrow." He reached for my hand as if to take it, then looked at Mary and dropped his hand. But I wanted him to take my hand. In fact, I wanted him to take me in his arms and hold me.

"Okay," I said quietly, dropping my eyes to the floor.

"Farewell, lass," he said.

"Bye." I didn't look up as I struggled with rising anxiety that made my heart pound.

I saw Calum's feet leave my field of vision and then heard the door open and close.

"Come on then," Mary said briskly. "I have work to do and must hurry." She bustled across the room, opened an impossibly narrow door and sidestepped through it, given the fullness of her figure and skirts. I followed her mutely, disliking her intensely. With any shred of kindness, she might have made the situation work for me, but no, I couldn't stay.

We stepped into a dark hallway that ended in a steep set of stairs. As if we climbed a ladder, we ascended the narrow wooden stairs until we reached a small landing.

"Here ye be." Mary opened a single door on the landing and stood back. As short as I was, I had to bend to enter the room. I had once seen an attic bedroom in a turn-of-the-century American row house belonging to a high school friend of mine. It had seemed spacious yet cozy. This room, in comparison, was about the same size as the walk-in closet in my apartment in a Seattle suburb. And I had thought that was too small.

Thankfully, at five feet two inches, I could straighten...barely. Mary declined to follow me in. She was taller. And her hips were very wide. Could she have even fit in the room?

"There is a bed, a chair and a dresser. I will send one of the lasses up with one of my old dresses."

With that, she whirled around and left the room. I turned and eyed the tiny sagging mattress covered by a thick gray blanket. A cracked pot peeped out from underneath the bed.

The chair, figuratively on its last legs, had been placed by the head of the bed, and a scratched and dented wooden dresser lined the opposite wall.

Thankfully, a tiny window above the bed provided a small measure of light. I climbed up on the saggy mattress with a cautious step to see if I could open it and air the stuffy room out, but the latch didn't budge. I sighed and lowered myself to a sitting position, pressing my back against the cold plaster wall.

"Oh, no," I said dispiritedly. "This isn't going to work. I can't sit here all day."

I had planned to take off as soon as Calum left the inn but now decided I should wait to change into a dress so I could pass for eighteenth century should someone see me.

For the next half hour, I twiddled my thumbs and stared at the walls, feeling thoroughly abandoned by my Highland hero, until one of the girls knocked on the door and entered, lugging a pitcher of steaming water in one hand and a mass of gray-and-white material in her other arm.

Petite, and appearing to be about sixteen or so, the slender brunette dipped a curtsey. I jumped up to grab the pitcher of water from her and set it down next to a plain white ceramic washbasin on the dresser. For a moment, she eyeballed my jeans even more closely than she had in the kitchen, before looking up to speak to me.

"Mrs. MacDowell sent me up with some water and a dress for ye, miss." A red nose and watery blue eyes indicated some sort of illness or allergies.

"Thank you," I said. "What's your name?"

"Kathleen, miss." She laid the clothing across the bed, the volume of which engulfed the small mattress. I saw the reason for Mary's wide skirts. A once-white donut-shaped padded roll lay on top of the mass of material on the bed. I turned to study Kathleen's skirts. Although she appeared to be underweight, her slender waist curved into improbably full hips. I looked down at the padded roll on the bed again and then back at Kathleen, memorizing the placement of her clothing.

"Linen and soap are in the top dresser drawer," Kathleen said with a curtsy as she turned to leave.

"Thank you, Kathleen," I said. I would have loved to call her back to tell me how to dress, but I thought better of it. As Calum said, I really didn't need to stand out.

The door shut behind her, and I didn't have far to move to reach the dresser, a matter of a few feet really. I pulled open the top drawer and withdrew a fairly dingy linen cloth that I guessed was supposed to serve as a towel. A lump of something equally gray, which I imagined was supposed to be soap, lay at the bottom of the dusty drawer.

I poured some hot water into the bowl and tried to lather up the soap. Failing that, I settled for rinsing my hands and face. Dabbing my cheeks dry with the towel, I turned around to regard the clothing on the bed.

I had only to set the towel down and cross the room in two or three steps to reach the garments. I sorted through the pile, which featured an off-white linen shift that had seen better days, a similarly colored petticoat, the hip-roll thingy, a cotton corset that tied in the front, a pale-gray cotton bodice jacket with three-quarter sleeves, and a darker charcoal gray overskirt.

I looked down at my own clothing, my long-sleeve blouse and my jeans, and I decided that although I might have to get rid of my blouse, I was going to keep my jeans on. I didn't see why not. I slipped out of my blouse and my bra, and slid the plain shift over my head, pulling the drawstrings tight to cinch the neckline up high above my cleavage.

I picked up the roll and studied it. From the strings in the front, I assumed I was supposed to tie it around my waist. But if I put the roll on my hips first, how would I get the corset on?

With a sigh, I picked up the corset and wrapped it around my waist. I pulled the faded-blue crisscrossed ribbons tight across my chest, but not so tightly that I couldn't breathe. It didn't feel as miserable as I thought it might. I tried bending over, as if to pick something up from the floor.

No! No bending, at least not to forty-five degrees. It didn't hurt. It simply didn't happen.

I picked up the padding again and tied it around my waist. Once tied, I felt foolish with nowhere to put my arms. They no longer hung loosely at my sides but, due to the roll on my hips, were forced away from my body in an unnatural angle. I crooked my arms and rested my elbows on the padding with a grin. I supposed in the future I would have to clasp my hands together in a devout posture. No wonder ladies in historical paintings looked so pious.

I rotated slowly, wondering if I was going to manage to get back out the door with my now buxom figure. And there was still more clothing to go!

I picked up the dark-gray skirt and studied it. The only way possible into the skirt was too slide it over my head, which I did, securing it with laces behind me. Thick and stiff, the skirt hung heavy on top of my jeans, the shift, the corset and the hoop. Given the weight of the clothing, I wasn't sure I could walk two steps, much less sneak down the stairs and out of the building.

At long last, the ugly blanket covering the mattress found its way to the light as I picked up the final garment, the bodice. As I did so, a stiff piece of material fell to the floor, and I tried to bend over to pick it up. The corset didn't yield, and I resorted to bending my knees and scooping the thing up. I had no idea where it went, but I was fairly sure I wasn't going to undress anytime soon if it was an undergarment of some kind.

Although I slipped the bodice jacket over my head easily enough, the garment must have been too small, as I couldn't tie the thick faded-black ribbons tightly enough to close the front across my chest.

I tugged at both sides of the bodice, hoping for some stretch, but with no luck. I wondered if I should creep down to the kitchen and ask Kathleen what to do. My eyes fell on the thick triangular quilted piece I'd picked up from the floor, and I lifted it off the bed to study it again. The top was wide, and it tapered down to a *V* shape. I tried to remember what the landlady's bodice looked like. Had it closed properly in the front? Kathleen's dress had been a one-piece affair—no ribbons for the kitchen cooks.

I eyed the piece in my hand again and, on a whim, stuffed it down the front of the bodice. A perfect fit, the top stopped at the neckline and the bottom came to a point in front of my stomach. I grinned. Yes! What a clever girl I was!

With no mirror small enough to fit in the miniscule room, I had no idea what I looked like, but I wasn't sure that I cared. The landlady had provided no shoes, and that was fine with me. I intended to continue wearing my comfortable athletic shoes.

At long last, dressed in period-appropriate clothing, there was no reason to delay my escape. I took a deep breath, eased the door open and listened carefully. I heard the voices of the cooks and the distinct sounds of pots and pans banging in the kitchen. I strategized about how best to get out of the building.

My plan of escape hadn't been particularly well thought out, and I supposed I should have waited until the pub was closed for the night to sneak out. But I was dressed, I was determined, and I was going.

I tiptoed downstairs, heedless of the creaking wood stair treads. The kitchen was far too noisy for anyone to hear me. The sound of men's voices and laughter caught my ears, and I assumed that noise was coming from the pub. The question most pressing was whether I should turn left toward the kitchen or right toward the pub in order to get out of the building as fast as possible. No matter what I decided, I was going to have to hustle.

Opting for the kitchen and hoping for the best, I opened the door at the bottom of the steps and peeked out to scan the kitchen. Mary was nowhere to be seen, and Kathleen and the other young cook had their backs to me. Luck was on my side, and I pushed the door open wide and prepared to run.

Running in heavy eighteenth-century skirts with preposterously wide hips was easier said than done. I barely squeezed through the small doorway leading from the attic, and once I did, all I could do was waddle to the kitchen toward the back door as my skirts swayed with a life of their own.

My heart pounded against the rigid corset, but I made it through the kitchen and out the door without being seen—at least not by the cooks.

I stopped short at the bustling scene in front of me. What I had thought to be a quiet and isolated alley behind the inn was in reality a hub of activity. Several wagons rolled past me, and I pressed myself up against the building, trying unsuccessfully to hide.

I should have known the stables would be behind the inn. Hadn't I seen the boy take the horses back there? And hadn't I seen the soldiers follow him to be housed in the stables?

And apparently, they hadn't left yet. My heart stopped when I saw the familiar bright-red jackets of the English soldiers as they milled about. The last thing I wanted to do was run into Lieutenant Dunston. It was too late to turn around and go back inside, and I didn't want to anyway. I would have killed for a shawl to drape over my head or some Gothic black cloak in which to conceal myself, but I was out of luck.

I raised a hand to my face when I saw Sergeant Wilson emerge from the stables. He stood with his hands on his hips, surveying the scene. He turned in my direction, and I lowered my head, grabbed up my skirts and turned right to hurry away, hoping that no one called out to me. Because if he did, I was running for it anyway.

I trotted around the side of the building and peered around the front.

The street was fairly empty except for two men who entered the inn. Fortunately, I didn't think they'd seen me.

Knowing I couldn't stand there long, I drew in a deep breath and held it as I sprinted away from the inn toward the road.

I turned left and moved as fast as I could away from the village and back down the path toward the river, toward the hills where Calum's cottage lay. Keeping my ears attuned to the sound of shouts behind me, I heard none.

In the chaos of the past few hours, I had given some thought to what I would do and where I would go once I left the inn. I simply had no options, nowhere to go, no way of making a living.

I was going to try one last time to return to the twenty-first century, and failing that, I was going to return to the hills and beg Calum to reconsider and let me stay up there. If he refused, I would have to find a way to hide out in the hills and try to live off the land. As ridiculous as that sounded, it was really the only other option I thought I could tolerate. I couldn't live in the attic of the public inn under the eye of a woman who despised me.

Still worried that the sergeant might have seen me, I looked over my shoulder often and kept up a steady pace along the trail, dragging my skirts along with me. I wasn't quite sure what I intended to do if someone chased after me—maybe take a nosedive into the grass on the right side of the road, but I couldn't imagine that anyone would fail to see me and my big poufy skirts popping out from the brush.

I wasn't sure of the time, but I guess it was around two in the afternoon. Given that it was September, the days were shorter, and I wasn't sure how much time I had before it turned dark. I definitely wasn't sure that I could make it up into the hills before nightfall.

I kept moving, my hips aching from the weight of the clothing. I stumbled often but managed to stay on my feet. When I felt like I had marched for about half an hour, I scanned the riverbank looking for the particular spot where I had arrived.

I froze. A man kneeled on the bank of the river. My pulse quickened.

Calum!

There was nowhere to hide and nothing I could do to escape detection. I tried to block the image of him forcibly dragging me back to the village. He wouldn't do that, would he?

Calum looked up.

"Lass!"

I unlocked my legs and moved forward slowly, reaching his side as he stood.

"Calum." I wasn't sure what else to say.

"Och, lass! Where are ye going?" My cheeks flushed as he examined me from head to foot.

"I can't stay there," I said with a shake of my head. I self-consciously wrapped my arms around my waist and placed a not-too-casual hand over the neckline of my bodice.

"But why?"

I shrugged. "I just can't stand it there. I don't know what to say. I was going to try to travel back to the twenty-first century one more time. And if that failed, I was going to beg you to let me stay up in the hills." I clasped my hands together as I pled my case.

"If you really, truly can't see yourself allowing me to stay with you, and if I can't figure out how to get back to my own time, then I'll figure out a way to survive in the woods." I dropped my eyes to the ground, knowing that I had put Calum in a very difficult position. He seemed like a very chivalrous man, and I felt for him.

"What am I going to do with ye, lass? What am I going to do with ye?"

I shook my head.

"I don't know, Calum. I'm so sorry to put you in this position, but I'm not going back."

Calum reached up and touched my shoulder briefly before dropping his hand.

"I am so verra sorry. Was it so bad?"

"It was pretty hideous, Calum. The room was a closet, and Mary was a witch."

"A witch?" Calum's eyes narrowed.

"No, no, not *that* kind of witch!" I smiled faintly. I had to remember that I had landed in a very superstitious era, and bandying the word "witch" about was probably not something I should make a habit of.

"I just meant that she really, really didn't like me, Calum. That wasn't going to change."

Calum's lips twitched, and a smile touched the corner of his eyes. He nodded.

"Is it yer intent then to test the waters one more time?" He looked toward the river, and I followed his gaze.

"Yes, I think I should."

"Ye must do as ye see fit. I will no stand in yer way."

And he literally took a few steps back.

I swallowed hard.

"Here we go again!" I said with a bright smile. I was so happy to see Calum again that I wasn't absolutely sure I wanted to head back so soon after all.

I approached the bank and hitched my skirts up over my knees to kneel down. I thought I heard Calum clear his throat, but I wasn't sure. I opted not to turn around, because I thought if I did, I might change my mind and stay in the eighteenth century.

With a pounding heart, I bent over and scooped up some icy water to splash on my face, hoping that it wouldn't tingle, that it wouldn't make me dizzy, that it wouldn't take me away from Calum.

He did not rush forward to grab my hand, as he had. He didn't touch me in any way.

And I didn't travel. Nothing happened. Again.

Rather than cold tingling, a warm sense of relief flooded through my body, and I had to admit that I wasn't ready to go yet. I wasn't ready to say good-bye to Calum.

I struggled to my feet, and at that, Calum did hurry forward to help me up.

"Still here!" I pronounced with a crooked smile.

Calum laughed, a wonderfully melodic sound that curled my toes.

"So ye are," he said. He held out his arm to me. "Shall we?"

With bright cheeks, I tucked my hand up under his arm and allowed him to lead me away from the river and toward my future.

Chapter Seven

Calum half pushed/half carried me up the steep trail into the hills. I had thought our earlier ascent was hard in my jeans, but with the added weight and length of the heavy skirts, I struggled even more.

We crested the hill, and I paused, trying to bend over to catch my breath, but failing given the rigidity of the bodice. It was an odd moment of revelation. Why did we bend over to catch our breath? I would have to do so with perfect posture, something that was probably easier on our lungs anyway.

"I didna imagine when I asked Mary to lend ye a gown that we would be climbing these hills again." Calum said. He slipped an arm around my waist and let me lean on him while I tried to breathe through my aching ribs.

"The first thing I'm going to do when we get back is get out of this outfit."

Then I remembered.

"Oh, no! I left my blouse behind!"

"And yer trews," Calum said.

"Oh, no! Not my jeans." I lifted my skirt and thrust out a blue-jeaned leg.

Calum laughed again, that wonderfully hearty sound I had heard earlier.

"Why am I no surprised?" he said. "I can give ye a shirt, though it will be quite large on ye. And I will try to pick up yer blouse the next time I go down to the village."

"Oh, shoot! What's Mary going to say to you? About me taking off?"

"Taking off? Dinna tell me ye left without telling her."

"Ummm...actually, I did. Snuck right out."

Calum, still supporting me, shook his head.

"I will have to tell her something. I ken she will suspect ye left of yer own free will, that naethin untoward happened to ye."

I sighed.

"And she'll keep your money. I'm so sorry, Calum. I could have told her I wasn't staying and asked for a portion of the money back, leaving her some for the clothing."

"Nay," he said. "We dinna do things that way. Do ye do such in yer time?"

"Ask for money back if we leave a hotel early?" I nodded. "Yes, quite often." I was probably recovered enough to move out of his arms, but I really didn't want to.

Unfortunately, Calum removed his arm and stepped back.

"Do ye feel well enough to continue?"

I nodded. He held out his arm, and I took it again as we followed the trail through the meadow. The sound of the sheep bleating caught my ear, and I smiled happily at the alpine feel of the whole thing. The last time Calum had brought me up here, it had been night. Now, the late afternoon sun highlighted the foliage changing from green to rust. And I wasn't afraid anymore. I didn't know what my future would hold, but I wasn't afraid. Not if Calum was there.

We entered his cabin, and after Calum slipped out of his coat, he immediately hooked a pot over the iron frame in the fireplace.

"Are ye hungry?" he asked.

"Always," I said with a bright smile. I moved to sit down on the dining table chair but had no idea how to position myself so I could actually hit the narrow seat in my wide skirts without ending up on the floor. I put a hand on the chair back and contemplated my next move.

"Please sit. Ye must be tired," Calum said as he returned to the table with the ubiquitous ale and tankards.

"Yes," I said. I bit my lip and eyed the chair again. No, my wide hips were never going to fit on that tiny chair.

"The thing is..." I took a deep breath. "I'm going to have to get out of this skirt. There's no way I can stuff *this* outfit onto *that* chair."

Calum stopped in the middle of pouring the ale and stared at me with rounded eyes. I knew I shocked him sometimes, but I couldn't help it.

"So I think I'm just going to slide out of this stuff, if you don't mind." I reached for the drawstrings at my waist, and Calum dropped the tankard with a clatter.

"Here? Now?" he whispered, looking around as if we stood in the middle of a crowded room.

"I've got my jeans on, remember? Besides, it's not like you have a bathroom I can change in."

Like a flash, he was at the door. "I will await ye outside. Call me when ye are ready." He shut the door behind him, and I divested myself of my skirts, petticoat and the padding. My shift fell down to my knees, and I contemplated its length. I suspected that one of Calum's shirts would be equally long, given that he was about a foot taller than me, maybe more.

I unlaced my bodice and corset with determination. I had no intention of wearing the stiff garments around in the woods. Why bother? I grabbed up the hem of my shift, hoisted it up to my waist and tied one side into a knot, a la oversized T-shirt style. I tightened the drawstring on the neckline of the shift, mourned the loss of my bra, which I'd left along with my blouse, and pronounced myself as satisfied with the results as I could be.

"Okay, Calum, you can come in," I called out as I bent to grab up the clothing from the floor. I carried it to the bed to attempt to fold it.

Calum entered and eyed me. With heated cheeks, I turned around to face him, suddenly self-conscious about my improvised blouse.

He smiled and nodded, returning to the table to finish pouring the ale.

"I see ye have managed without one of my shirts," he said.

"Yes, I think it will do for now, right? Covers everything." I looked down at my neckline to make sure that it did. The material was thick enough to keep from clinging to my body.

"Aye," he said. "Ye look well enough."

I took that as a compliment and finished bunching up the clothing I had removed into some sort of order. I set it next to the tartan blanket Calum had covered me with the night before, and I returned to the table to sit down. I picked up my ale and took a sip of the hearty warm liquid.

"So, how do you make a living up here, Calum? I know I've hinted around at the question before, but I don't think you've answered."

Calum, back to stirring the pot, looked over his shoulder.

"Ye are an inquisitive lass. Is this common in yer time?"

"Yes, and don't try to distract me."

"But is it no considered rude to ask people about money?"

"Yes. Calum, please."

He paused, and I thought he wasn't going to answer.

"My family had lands, an ancestral home, wealth. I lost my home and my lands, but I collected as much money as I could before I had to leave." His voice dropped to a deep baritone, his words clearly affecting him deeply.

They also brought an ache to my throat.

"Oh, Calum, I'm so sorry."

Calum gave the pot a last stir and turned around to take the seat across the table from me. He drank some ale before responding.

"It was my fault," he said. His face darkened in a morose expression as he contemplated his tankard.

"How?" I was afraid to cause him further unhappiness, but I persisted.

"The Crown confiscated my lands and home."

"Why?"

"I fought at Culloden. Most of the lairds who fought in the rebellion lost their lands, titles, wealth."

I drew in a sharp breath. The first thing that struck me was joy that he survived the battle. The second was the word "lairds."

"Oh!" I released my breath. "I didn't know."

"Nor would ye. Verra few lairds who fought at Culloden lived to tell the story."

"Lairds? Do you mean lords? Are you an aristocrat?"

"In name only these days. I am a titled laird." He leaned forward. "I tell ye this in secrecy, lass. There is a price on my head."

I gasped. "The English? But what about the soldiers? Lieutenant Dunston? You sat right behind him in the pub. How could you go into the pub knowing you could get caught? Are you one of the Jacobites he and his men were searching for?"

Calum leaned back in his chair and drank. He set his tankard down and nodded.

"Aye, they seek me as well as others."

"How could you risk going into the pub? When I first saw you, you were just relaxing, enjoying a beer!"

He smiled evenly.

"I was no relaxed, lass, but I didna think it wise to flee the room when the lieutenant and his sergeant entered."

"And then I threw myself on you, bringing you to their attention." I shuddered and shook my head at my foolishness.

Calum leaned across the table and covered my hand with his own. A breathtaking warmth spread up my arm at the contact.

"It was no yer fault, lass. Ye didna ken."

I appreciated his words, but I still blamed myself for putting him in danger.

"So you really are hiding up here? Is this on your land?"

He shook his head.

"Nay. This is an old shepherd's cottage which belongs to a cousin of mine. My land lies beyond the hills at the far end of this valley. My former land, that is. My family's ancestral home, Castle Heuvan, lies on the shores of Loch Heuvan."

Again, I heard the pain in his voice. I marveled at the thought that his family home had been a castle. Now I understood why he had those delicate teacups. They had probably come from his home.

"Does your cousin know you're here?"

He nodded. "Aye, he does. His wife has the way of ye. I ken she is from the Colonies as well."

I barely heard his words, imaging a beautiful castle on the shores of a lake.

"It must be so hard to be close to your home but not able to see it."

"I have returned to it, albeit in the dark of night. I dinna wish to be discovered. My retainers still farm the land for the Crown, and I believe they would be loyal to me, but I dinna wish to place them in harm's way. My house has been stripped. Most things of value were carted away by English soldiers. I took a few small things, whatever I could carry in my pocket."

Calum's voice deepened in bitterness, and he rose quickly and turned his back, ostensibly to check the food cooking in the hearth. His shoulders, normally broad and even, drooped.

I wished I could do something to help. Me, from the twenty-first century, with all the knowledge we possessed. What could I do to help?

Rather than murmur empty words of sympathy, I pressed my lips together and watched as he ladled yet another stew onto plates and served them with oatcakes.

Calum resumed his seat and applied himself to his food. I nibbled on mine, hot and delicious, but my appetite had evaporated. He obviously didn't want to talk—at least not about his lands—and I found it difficult to focus on anything particularly mundane, like the weather. There was so much I wanted to know about him, but all my questions would probably be unwelcome.

Calum surprised me by talking.

"I miss my home. I miss my lands. I failed the tenants living on my land, some who have lived there for hundreds of years. All are part of my clan, my family's clan." Calum set his spoon down and sat back in his chair, one finger idly tracing the pattern in the wooden table.

"I believed we had a chance to drive the English from our country. I believed in Prince Charlie's cause to restore a Scot to the throne. I kent there was a chance we might lose, but I ignored my instincts. My father joined the Old Pretender, James, in the Fifteen, when I was a wee babe in my mother's arms.

"When it became clear that James could no win, he left Scotland for France. My father went with him, ne'er to return. He died of the flux on the passage. I told ye an untruth about that, and I apologize. I didna ken ye at the time, and as I am a wanted man, I dinna trust easily."

Calum's frown deepened.

"I understand," I said. "Is your mother still alive then?"

"Nay. My mother grew bitter with my father's loss, and although the Indemnity Act of 1717 allowed us to keep our land and home, she never forgave the English. She died some years ago, always dreaming that young Prince Charlie would come home and claim his throne. I sought to honor her memory."

A hot tear slipped down my cheek, and I surreptitiously wiped it away. Thankfully, Calum kept his eyes on the table and didn't see my sadness.

"There was no Indemnity Act this time, no pardon, at least no for me."

"I'm so sorry, Calum."

He nodded, his eyes focused on a spot on the table.

"Thank ye. It is, as I said, my fault."

"Still."

He sighed and raised his tankard to his lips.

"Perhaps I will take ye to see the old place."

"Is there any chance you can buy it back? Pay a penalty?"

"It is more likely the Crown would hang me than negotiate."

"There really are no more rebellions, you know. I don't remember much about Scottish history, but I do think Culloden was the last rebellion against the English."

At that, Calum looked up, his eyes hardening. I couldn't believe that I'd knowingly pressed that hot button again. I hoped he wasn't about to storm out, but he eyed me steadily.

"Are ye saying that Scotland will never be free of England?"

I was in over my head on that one. I understood nothing of Scottish politics.

"No, I don't think so."

Calum tossed back the rest of his ale and poured more. He drank half of that before setting it down on the table with a bang. I took a swig of my own ale, watching him warily. This wasn't a side of Calum I had seen before.

He looked up at me, and his features softened.

"I have frightened ye," he said.

"A little bit," I said with a weak smile.

"Forgive me, lass. Tell me more of the future. Tell me of your home."

For the next few hours, long after he rose to light candles, I told Calum about my home in a suburb of Seattle, my work as a photographer, my now deceased parents and status as an only child. We shared that in common, it seemed. Calum too was an only child, his mother having never remarried.

He asked questions about the future, and I answered as best I could. I reassured him that the people of Scotland seemed happy enough as members of the United Kingdom and that they had their own parliament.

He was particularly fascinated with my description of the United States, all fifty of them, and the War of Independence, freeing the country from British colonialism.

"Why didn't you leave Scotland?" I asked. "Why don't you leave now? Find a life in the United States?"

Calum tilted his head and eyed me with a hint of a smile.

"The 'United States' disna exist just yet, lass. The Colonies *are* ruled by the English. I would still be a wanted man."

"Oh! That's right." I frowned. "So you're staying in Scotland? In hiding for the rest of your life?"

"It is my home," he said softly. "And if I should leave? What would happen to ye?"

"Oh, gosh, don't think about staying just to take care of me."

He leaned forward again, taking my hand in his.

"Lass, dinna discount how much danger ye are in yerself. Yer presence is suspect. Ye canna explain yerself, where ye come from, who ye are. Time traveling will only be regarded as witchcraft here, and witches dinna historically fare well in Scotland."

The concern in his eyes touched me, and it frightened me at the same time. What *was* I going to do?

I covered his hand with my own.

"Well, we're a pair, aren't we?" I murmured. "I suppose we could both hide out up here forever."

"Och, lass, I wouldna wish that for ye. I wish ye to have a happy life. How can ye find happiness up here in a tiny cottage in a land far, far away from yer own home, yer own time?"

I studied Calum's dark shoulder-length hair, wishing I could run my fingers through the silky-looking curls. Was he crazy? What women wouldn't give up everything to live in a cottage in the mountains with the handsome Highlander?

But I didn't say that.

"I seem to be stuck here for now." I hurried to amend my words. "And I'm grateful to you for allowing me to stay."

"Stuck is probably most apt, lass," he said with a wry smile.

Calum looked up toward the window and rose to light some candles and a lantern, though the fire amply lit the small cabin, leaving few shadows.

"The sun is setting," he said. "Ye look weary. Perhaps an early night."

I gulped and looked over at the bed.

Calum grinned, showing bright-white teeth.

"Dinna fash, lass. I shall sleep here on the floor, as I did last night."

With a chuckle, he picked up the dishes as I rose, with embarrassed cheeks, from my seat.

"Of course," I said. "I'm just going to go outside and..."

Calum looked over his shoulder and smiled.

"Take the lantern to light the way."

I picked up the lantern and stepped outside, shutting the door behind me. Twilight had descended in the hills, and a few stars twinkled in the dark-lavender sky.

The sheep seemed abnormally noisy, bleating more than usual. I didn't know when lambing season was, but I didn't think it would be in September. Holding the lantern high, I headed away from the cabin, following the trail into the woods.

I found a likely spot and set the lantern down. Just as I was about to unzip my jeans, I heard a rustling in the nearby brush, and I froze.

"Calum?" I called out. Not likely. I suspected it was probably a rabbit or something. I listened for any repeat noise but heard nothing. Even the sheep had quieted.

"Silly bunny," I mumbled before turning my attention to my jeans again.

"Before you go too much further, Miss Brown, I think we must announce our presence," a disembodied and familiarly languid voice announced from the gathering darkness.

Chapter Eight

I gasped and tried to whirl around but found myself caught in the grasp of two English soldiers, each holding on to my arms.

"Let me go!" I shrieked. "What are you doing?"

Lieutenant Dunston moved toward me, Sergeant Wilson at his right hand. His pale face flickered in the light of my lantern. So Sergeant Wilson *had* seen me! Somehow, they had managed to follow us.

"Miss Brown, please do not fight the men," Lieutenant Dunston said. "You will only suffer injury."

"What are you doing?" I ground out. "What is this?"

"Sergeant Wilson alerted me that he saw you leaving the inn today, dressed quite differently than when you arrived. At first I thought to dismiss the matter entirely, but there is something about you that piques my curiosity. And the gentleman who escorted you out of the inn last night, the one you met by the river today. Your landlord, I believe you called him?"

His wrinkled nose suggested he hadn't believed that Calum was my landlord.

"Yes, and rather than lose sight of you, Sergeant Wilson quite rightly sent a man to follow you before alerting me and organizing the men. When we caught up to him, he was able to report back to me with your very odd activities. And of your cozy little cottage up here in the hills."

He looked around the woods.

"I cannot tell you how many times we have searched this valley before but did not spot the cottage. How many times, Sergeant Wilson? Four? Five?"

"Yes, sir," the sergeant replied accommodatingly. He eyed me almost apologetically.

I struggled in the hold of the two soldiers but could not break free of their grasp. My heart pounded so loudly in my ears I could barely hear the lieutenant's words. Tears streamed down my face, and I couldn't wipe them away. I had to escape. I just had to.

"What do you want with me?"

"Not just you, my dear, but your landlord. I am most curious about him, most curious."

"Curious?" I eked out through trembling lips.

"Yes, Miss Brown. Curious. Your 'landlord' stated he was a tenant farmer and that you leased a cottage on his property. Surely no crops can be grown at this elevation. I see no fields. What sort of farmer lives up here in the hills? He could more plausibly have said he was a shepherd, for that is the only industry up here. And yet he does not have the look of a shepherd either."

I pressed my lips together, though my instinct was to scream for help. I didn't want Calum to come for me. I wanted him to run away as far as he could.

Lieutenant Dunston waited for my answer, and upon seeing that I wasn't going to give him one, he clucked under his teeth.

"No matter, Miss Brown. We will discover the truth soon enough. Initially, I took little notice of your landlord last night. What was his name, Sergeant Wilson?"

"I am afraid I do not remember, sir."

"Calum Campbell!" the lieutenant exclaimed. "That is his name! I particularly remember commenting on how many Campbells were in the area. Yes, as I was saying, I took little notice of Mr. Calum Campbell in the pub last night, but when you ran to him with such unbridled enthusiasm, I began to wonder about him. Still, I was fatigued and unhappy that I could not make it back to the fort to recuperate but had instead to stay at that awful inn. I have not been well, you see.

"I ignored my instincts and let both of you go with minimal questioning. That is how I know that I am in need of rest. Sergeant Wilson has nagged at me long enough on the subject. To make such a mistake because I was peeved about the accommodations, well, that is simply unacceptable.

"However, when Sergeant Wilson fortuitously discovered that you had returned to the inn in altered attire and that you departed most furtively, I knew providence had smiled upon me, and the men and I set out to investigate. And now we have found your cottage."

"He's just my landlord," I muttered. "That's all."

"Yes, and is that cottage the one you have leased? If so, where does your Mr. Campbell live? Something does not sound quite right here, my dear. Shall we visit with him and discover the truth?"

One of his men lifted the lantern and preceded us as we made our way back to the cabin. I dragged my heels, forcing the soldiers to half carry me.

I frantically debated on whether or not I should scream for Calum to run. He would most likely not be able to make out my exact words of warning but would run toward us in response to my screams.

What could I do?

"Wait!" I called out loudly, hopefully loud enough for Calum to hear.

Lieutenant Dunston paused.

"Yes, Miss Brown?"

"Look, he really is my landlord, just a tenant farmer. I'm not sure what you're looking for, probably me. You probably know about me by now, don't you?" Of course, I wasn't making any sense, but was I loud enough for Calum to hear and make good an escape?

"What should we know about you, madam?"

"Well, that I'm a time—"

"Lieutenant!" Calum stopped me, entering the circle of light. "What are ye doing with Miss Brown? Please have yer men unhand her, sir."

"Ah, Mr. Campbell! Good evening. No, I think we will not unhand Miss Brown just yet." Lieutenant Dunston raised a hand, and two of the soldiers moved in to stand behind Calum. Calum looked over his shoulders at the men.

"I am the one ye want, Lieutenant, not Miss Brown."

At Calum's capitulation, the soldiers took him by the arms. A sob escaped my lips.

"Yes, I think I do want you, Mr. Campbell. But I think we also want Miss Brown."

"She has done nothing wrong."

"No, perhaps not," the lieutenant said thoughtfully. "But there is something very incongruous about her, do you not think? And she was just about to disclose something to us, something of importance. What was that, my dear?"

I threw a frightened look toward Calum, who shook his head.

"Nothing. I can't remember what I was going to say."

"Cannot remember? Perhaps I can refresh your memory? It had something to do with time?"

"Lieutenant, I didna wish to speak poorly of Miss Brown, especially no in front of her," Calum said with a pointed glance in my direction, "but she is a bit off her head, if ye ken my meaning. I did rent the cottage to her, but I think I must return her to her cousins in Glasgow."

"Glasgow!" the lieutenant repeated with a lift of his eyebrows. "Well, that is the first I have heard of this Glasgow scheme. Come, you two. Let us venture into this cottage of yours and see if you can provide some refreshment while we sort this out. In the morning, you will accompany us back to the fort, Mr. Campbell. And I think we must take you as well, Miss Brown, if we cannot resolve your origins before then. I cannot in all conscience simply leave you up here in the wild Highlands to fend for yourself. No, I truly cannot."

Lieutenant Dunston shook his head in a poor attempt to simulate concern. I heartily doubted that he was worried about my safety.

We returned to the cottage, Calum and I struggling with and resisting our captors to no avail. The two soldiers holding Calum pushed him inside. Lieutenant Dunston nodded to my two handlers, and they released me. I followed Calum in, and the lieutenant and sergeant entered behind me.

"Wait outside," Lieutenant Dunston called over his shoulder to the rest of the men. Sergeant Wilson shut the door.

"Please sit, Mr. Campbell, Miss Brown." The soldiers forced Calum into a chair and stood back. With shaky legs, I lowered myself to the seat. Lieutenant Dunston took a third chair, but Sergeant Wilson stood by the door.

I watched as the lieutenant set his hat down on the table and surveyed the room, and I followed his eyes to the bed. He rose suddenly and crossed over to the bed to bend down and study the tartan blanket. A quick glance at Calum revealed that he watched the lieutenant warily. Was any tartan forbidden or just his kilt? Or was it only *wearing* the kilt that was banned? Surely, every Highland woman did not need to throw her blankets out, did she? I wondered where Calum's kilt was. It was not readily visible.

"Yes, nice weaving," Lieutenant Dunston murmured without touching the material. I assumed he was too fastidious to touch strange blankets. "I am afraid I do not know clan tartans. Are these Campbell colors?"

"Aye," Calum murmured briefly.

The lieutenant then moved to study the clothing I had piled on the bed next to the blanket. He whirled around.

"Ah! Could this be your gown, Miss Brown, the one Sergeant Wilson reported he saw you wearing today?" he asked.

"The color is similar, sir," Sergeant Wilson offered in a muted voice. He cleared his throat.

The lieutenant ignored him. "I wonder that you decided to forgo proper clothing once again and return to wearing your trousers. Is it your habit to wear men's clothing, Miss Brown?"

I looked toward Calum, not knowing what to say. Were we really discussing my clothes? Calum eyed me steadily, but if he was sending me guidance, I didn't know what it was.

"Well, yes," I said. "It's just more comfortable, you know? And there's no one in the hills to care." I was hoping my chatty tone would disarm the lieutenant.

He studied me for a moment while I inwardly squirmed but outwardly met his gaze, albeit with a deer-in-the-headlight stare.

"No, it *is* very isolated up here, is it not? Which is why some of the Jacobite rebels have taken refuge in these hills." He turned to look at Calum.

"I wouldn't know about that," I piped up, trying to deflect his attention away from Calum. "I can't imagine my landlord knows about that either."

"No?" the lieutenant asked, his eyes shifting to me with a look of skepticism. He turned his attention back to Calum. "Where is your home exactly, Mr. Campbell, this land that you farm? And your wife? She does not mind that you seemed intent on staying the night at Miss Brown's cottage? What an accommodating woman, to be sure."

I dared not say anything. I wanted to say that there was no missus, that Calum was going to spend the night with me, but I had no idea what the laws were regarding such matters. I would have outed Calum as a liar, initiating even more suspicion, and then there was the adultery issue. I was pretty sure eighteenth-century Scotland was a bit more parochial about such things.

"My home is nearby," Calum answered dryly. "I had no intention of staying the night but intended to return to my home once I had surveyed the repairs needed on the roof."

The lieutenant quirked an eyebrow.

"In the dark?"

"I am no afraid of the dark."

"And you, Miss Brown? You really stay up here in the cottage alone? Without companion? Without protection?"

"Sure do." I nodded vehemently. "I'm from the Colonies, you know. That's what we do."

Lieutenant Dunston drew his sandy brows together with a faint smile in my direction. I knew I was confusing him with my nonsense. Was it enough?

"I find that hard to believe, Miss Brown, but in truth, I have never met anyone from the Colonies. Perhaps things are vastly different there, as you say. Nevertheless, I still think I must take both of you to Fort William to undergo further inquiries."

My throat closed over, and I felt faint. Why did his use of the word "inquiries" sound more like "inquisition"?

"There is no need to take Miss Brown," Calum started to say, but he was interrupted by an imperious hand raised in his direction.

"That will be enough discussion, Mr. Campbell. Now it is much too late for us to descend to the valley tonight. We shall make for Fort William at first light. Miss Brown, my men are tired and in need of sustenance. Do you have anything they could sup on?"

Calum rose. "Miss Brown is tired from the day's journey. She has a pot of stew set by which I can serve yer men with her permission." He looked at me, and I nodded as if giving that permission.

"Yes, that will be most agreeable," the lieutenant said. "However, I think before we sup, Miss Brown should change her attire. I have already heard several ribald comments from the men regarding her state of dress, and I do not wish to subject her to yet more vulgar comment. I will, of course, speak to the men in the meantime, Miss Brown, but it would be prudent for you to dress more appropriately. I hope that I am incorrect in noting you are wearing an undergarment for a blouse? No, you really must change. I insist." The lieutenant made a moue of faint distaste and shook his head.

My jaw dropped, and I was just about to spit out a testy comment, when Calum caught my eye and shook his head. I pressed my lips together as the lieutenant rose and turned for the door.

"Mr. Campbell, shall we give Miss Brown some privacy?" Lieutenant Dunston indicated the door, and the men filed outside.

"This is ridiculous!" I muttered as I rose to grab up the clothing and furiously tied, pulled and laced myself into the restrictive costume. Fifteen minutes later, I perched precariously on the chair and awaited their return. I had no intention of letting them know that I had finished dressing. I called out an irate response to enter when a knock sounded on the door within a few minutes.

"Ah! Miss Brown, this attire suits you much more than the men's clothing. Very elegant indeed." The lieutenant's compliment was delivered in his typical languid manner and sounded as artificial as anything else he had said. I hardly cared about his opinion.

The next few hours involved me sitting in the chair and Calum serving up the rest of his wonderful stew and ale. I could hear the appreciation of the soldiers, who were apparently going to bed down outside with their blankets. I watched Calum with bemusement as he moved about the cottage. Thankfully, the lieutenant didn't ask why I wasn't hostessing in my own cottage and seemed to accept Calum's explanation that I was tired. If I thought the past few days had been surreal, they had just gotten much more bizarre.

If Lieutenant Dunston and Sergeant Wilson intended to stay, were they planning on sleeping inside? If so, where?

The lieutenant resolved that question at the end of the meal.

"A very good stew, Miss Brown. My compliments. If you would be so good as to provide Mr. Campbell with a blanket, he will sleep outside with us. We will leave you in peace."

With a quick look in Calum's direction, I rose and lifted the folded gray blanket from the bed.

Calum took the blanket and followed the men outside. One of the soldiers shut the door behind them. I heard the sergeant issuing orders and the general hum of men's voices. Out from under the watchful eye of the men, I realized that I still hadn't gone to the bathroom, the very thing I was attempting to do when the English soldiers startled me. But there was no way I was going to raise the issue, no way I was going to go outside and tell twenty or so men that I had to use the restroom.

I turned and searched under the bed for anything remotely resembling a pot, but could find nothing. I perched on the edge of the bed, tears slipping down my face as much from discomfort as fear and frustration. Perhaps if I cried more, I'd have to urinate less.

I squeezed my knees together and studied the cabin forlornly. It felt like a prison, and I wanted out. I wanted to leave, to get away. I hitched up my skirts and pushed myself back against the wall, pulling my knees up to my chest, no easy task with the padding around my waist. If anyone walked in, they would be certainly be shocked. Again, I didn't care.

I surprised myself by nodding off for a few moments before the bouncing of my head against the stone wall awakened me. I listened intently to the sounds outside, guessing that the men were settling, as the hum of voices had faded. The fire in the hearth still burned heartily, and I closed my eyes, unwilling to lay down, unwilling to put myself in such a vulnerable position. I wasn't even sure I could lay down with the roll around my waist, and there was no way I was going to climb out of my clothing again, only to have to paste it all back on again in the morning.

I awakened to the feeling of something warm over my mouth. A hand. I clawed at the hand, struggling to scream, to breathe. A heavy weight pressed against my body, now prone on the bed.

"Hush, lass. Dinna scream. It is I, Calum."

Struggling to see in the darkened cabin, I stopped fighting with the body lying across mine. Calum lightened his grip.

"What are you doing?" I hissed, angry because he had frightened me so badly. To my right, I saw the fire had died down, leaving only embers in the hearth.

"I am rescuing ye, lass, and myself. There is a good chance that if the English get us to Fort William, neither of us will see the light of day again. I am more worried for ye than I am for myself."

Calum shifted his body and rolled off of me, coming to stand by the bed. He held out a hand, and I took it.

"How are we going to get out of here?" I whispered. "How did you get away from the soldiers?"

"They were that tired that the two soldiers watching over me fell asleep. I wouldna want to be them in the morn when it is discovered that we are gone."

"Where are we going?"

Calum let go of my hand and moved over to the cupboard by the hearth to collect what little food remained after the soldiers had taken their fill. I watched as he shoved a few oatcakes and some vegetables into a cloth sack and then filled another seemingly waterproof bag with a bit of ale he had apparently withheld from the men.

He slipped out of his coat and slung the bags over his left shoulder before handing the coat to me.

"Don this. It is chilly tonight." While I slipped into his coat, he moved over to the bed and bent down to retrieve something I hadn't seen—a length of material. He draped it over his shoulders, securing the food and ale, and looped some of the material under his belt. I recognized his kilt. Apparently, it could be worn any which way he wanted.

I fiddled with the overly long sleeves of Calum's coat. He tsked, folded back the cuffs and took my hand, leading me not to the front door but toward the fireplace.

With a quick look over his shoulder, he lifted one end of the cupboard and pulled it away from the wall. I hadn't noticed a curtain behind the cupboard, but Calum lifted a rectangular grayish piece of burlap-type material to reveal a small wooden door.

I blinked. Who would have thought such a small cottage would have two doors?

"Won't they be watching the back?" I whispered.

"Nay, I counted the soldiers." Calum kept his voice low. "They are all asleep in the front of the cottage. I dinna ken they saw that the cottage has a back door. It is wee thing, hardly noticeable."

Calum lifted the latch and eased open the door, sticking his head outside to look around. Grabbing my hand once again, he ducked his head to clear the small door and pulled me with him as we tiptoed outside. I clutched at my skirts. A gentle wind blew through the trees, rustling the leaves, which masked our steps...and my anxious panting.

Calum led me away from the cottage, sometimes having to tug as I paused to look over my shoulder, terrified someone would shout "Hold there!"

Darkness surrounded us, the moon seemingly absent from the sky. I imagined it was probably overcast, as I saw no stars either. In this setting so far from twenty-first century electricity and lights, I should have been able to see stars.

I heard the bleating of the sheep as we moved through the trees. I wasn't sure where we were headed, but it seemed as if we traveled toward the far hills on the opposite end of the valley.

"Calum," I whispered, tugging at his hand. "Where are we going?"

"We canna stop to discuss it, lass. Trust me."

"I do," I said under my breath.

We kept on, and I was thankful for his coat. The night air *was* cool, and we had entered an area thick with mist. The moisture crept into my clothing.

"How can you see where you're going?" I whispered again. He moved through the dense mist with a sure step.

"I have been this way many times," he said. He gave my hand a reassuring squeeze, and I relaxed in his care. Calum was nothing if not competent.

At some point, we had emerged from the thickest part of the forest and followed the tree line. The moon peeped out long enough to show me that a meadow stretched away to our left. It seemed as if we had traveled for about an hour when Calum slowed and came to a stop. He shrugged his kilt off his shoulders, lowered his bags and set them on the ground. He offered me a drink of ale, which I accepted gratefully, though I had to drink from the bag. The ale, however, reminded me of something that had been painfully apparent for the past half hour. I still had to go to the bathroom.

"Calum, I have to…" I jerked my head in the direction of the woods. "I didn't get to go before the soldiers grabbed me."

"Are ye saying ye have no relieved yerself since yesterday? Och, lass, ye are made of stronger stuff than I. Go, go, but make haste."

I dashed off into the woods but not so far that I couldn't still see Calum. I ran behind a bush, struggled to simultaneously lift skirts and drops jeans at the same time, and finally emerged from the woods pain-free.

"Whew! I feel better," I said. "What's next?"

"We must descend an old steep and narrow sheep trail that is cut into the mountain face, which leads to the loch below. Stay behind me and close to the hillside. I wouldna bring ye down this way in the dark if I didna have to, but we canna wait until morn to flee the hills. I suspect Lieutenant Dunston kens who I am and will follow us."

"So, will you tell me where we're going now?"

"To Castle Heuvan."

No matter how surreal my experience had been to date, to hear Calum say that we were going to a castle still sent a thrill up my spine. I was such a tourist!

"But why are you going there if you know they're going to follow you? Didn't you say they watch the castle, looking for you?"

"Aye, I have no doubt that Lieutenant Dunston will follow us there. My family's butler is now the caretaker. He will look out for the soldiers, and we can hide when they come. I grew up in the castle. I ken many hiding places within its walls. If we have to hide for a few days while the English search for us, so be it. Tucker will see to our needs. I ken I can trust him with my life, though I hate to put him in danger."

"I'm not sure Lieutenant Dunston himself is going to follow you. I think he's sick, sick and tired. He just wants to go back to the fort...and England, maybe more than he wants to find you. But even if they don't find you this time, what about regular patrols? How many times can you hide in the castle before you're caught?"

"I have watched the soldiers venture down to the castle over the past year. They do so regularly and predictably, staying at the castle for a day or two before moving on. Perhaps they too, like the lieutenant, are sick and tired, weary of hunting for Jacobites." His expression was bitter.

"Nevertheless, there is nowhere else to go. I cannot impose myself upon my cousin any further. I cannot go to live at his house, not as a wanted man. To endanger not only him but also his wife and child is unthinkable. Until I discover a way to disentangle myself from the consequences of my actions, I must endure this life as a fugitive. It is not what I would wish for ye though, lass."

He sighed heavily. I didn't know what to say.

"Come. We must go," Calum said. "The sun will rise in a few hours."

He picked up the bags and shouldered them before slinging his kilt over the lot. He took my hand once again and led the way. Though I couldn't see two feet in front of me, I could feel the elevation change in the trail, and I knew we were descending. Thankfully, I couldn't see enough to be scared, but the trail felt very narrow. Whimsically, I hoped the sheep walked single. We moved slowly, staying close to the hillside. I looked out into the darkness to my right but could see little. Occasionally, the moon peeped out and reflected in what I assumed was a lake. The sight was beautiful and mystical.

"Is that a lake?" I asked.

"Aye, that is Loch Heuvan. Castle Heuvan rests on the shores of the loch."

"Oh my," I breathed.

We followed the trail for about an hour before it started to level. My knees ached from the long, albeit gradual descent. Once on level ground, Calum led me along a narrow path flanked by knee-high grasses of some sort.

The moon peeped out again, highlighting a massive structure that seemed to pop up out of nowhere. Silver stone glowed, and I paused to stare.

"Welcome to Castle Heuvan," Calum said. "Though it is no longer mine to welcome ye to." His voice deepened, growing husky.

"Oh, Calum," I said. "I'm so sorry. I can't imagine how you must feel."

"I kent the consequences of joining the rebellion," he said, clearing his throat. "Come. The only way into the castle is through the door leading into the courtyard. I dinna ken if Tucker locks the door. There is probably no need. I suspect the Crown has taken everything of value."

Again, I heard the emotion in his voice.

We moved on toward the castle. No lights shone in any windows, and I wasn't surprised. The hour was late, and the caretaker was probably asleep.

The castle appeared to be set up on a promontory, and we climbed a grassy knoll to arrive at a massive set of large wooden doors at the base of the castle wall, the size of which astounded me, as I guessed it was at least four or five stories high. The moon still peeping through the clouds seemed to perch just on top of one of the two castellated towers at the front of the castle.

Calum let go of my hand to lift the latch of the door, but it didn't budge. He let out a quiet curse and searched over his shoulder, as if looking for followers. We hadn't passed any houses or any other people, and I suspected we were very much alone. But if Calum felt the English would soon be hot on our heels, I believed him.

He raised his fist to pound on the door. In the silence of the night, the sound echoed terribly. No one answered, and he pounded once again.

Chapter Nine

At long last, a commotion on the other side of the door indicated someone had arrived.

"Who is it?" the voice boomed. "What do ye mean banging on the door at this time of night? If ye mean to avail yerself of the castle, come at a decent hour!"

"Tucker!" Calum called out in a voice just loud enough to penetrate the door. "Let me in."

"Yer lairdship?" the voice asked. The latch lifted, and the door swung open. A little old man holding a lantern aloft, thin white hair streaming to his shoulders, bowed before Calum. He seemed to have dressed in a hurry, because his dark jacket was haphazardly buttoned over what appeared to be a white nightshirt that fell to the knees of his dark trousers.

He set the lantern down and grabbed Calum's hands.

"Yer lairdship! Why have ye come? It isna safe for ye here. Soldiers were here only a few days ago looking for ye, asking for a portrait of ye. I've hidden all the family pictures in my room, ye ken."

Calum freed one of his hands and patted Tucker on the shoulder.

"I ken, Tucker. I ken, but the English found me in the hills. I canna stay there any longer." He turned to me. "This is Miss Brown. She needs our protection from the soldiers as well."

Tucker bowed in my direction, eyeing me curiously.

"Pleased to meet ye, madam. Come in, yer lairdship. Come in." The butler stepped back, picked up his lantern and allowed us through the door. We entered not a building but what seemed to be a courtyard, or so I assumed from the open skies and cobblestoned flooring.

"Are ye hungry, yer lairdship? Do ye wish something to eat? I dinna have much set aside, but ye're welcome to it."

"I have brought some food with me, Tucker. See what ye can do with the lot." Calum extricated himself from his kilt and handed the butler the bags of food and ale.

Tucker took the bags and nodded. "Give me a wee bit of time, and I can give ye something decent to eat. I will set a fire in the great room."

"No, dinna go to such trouble," Calum said. "We dinna want to light the building up for all to see. We will eat in the kitchen."

Tucker nodded and led the way across a courtyard about half the length of a football field, through another set of double wooden doors, smaller than those leading into the castle. I guessed we were entering the great room. The light of Tucker's lamp played eerily off the plaster walls, throwing shadows in the empty corners. The room was barren with the exception of two wooden benches and an old scarred rectangular table far too small for the size of the room.

"Ah! I see that they took the tables, the benches, the tapestries and the rugs. I assume they took the silver and the china?" The gravelly sound in Calum's baritone resonated with unhappiness.

Tucker, marching across the empty room on his way to what I assumed was the kitchen, paused and turned, his face darkening with grief.

"Aye, master. I couldna stop them. The soldiers escorted some merchants into the house and stood by while they carted everything away to auction. But as I said, I did manage to hide the family portraits, yers included."

"Thank ye, Tucker. That must be why the soldiers have no recognized me yet. Or perhaps they have. It is only a matter of time afore they discover who I am."

We passed through a very small arched wooden door at the side of the great room, the kind Calum had to duck to go through, and we entered a narrow stone passage that ultimately led into a fairly large kitchen.

Hardly warm and inviting, the kitchen was cold and damp, the smell wet and musty. Tucker set the lantern, food and ale down on a small rectangular table and rushed to start a fire in an oversized hearth.

Calum stared at the room.

"Even the kitchen table?"

Tucker, kneeling in front of the fire, looked over his shoulder.

"Aye, yer lairdship. They left a few pieces that they thought were too auld to sell, and I mended the old school table and chairs to put in here for my meals."

I eyed the small rectangular wooden table. Scratched and dented, several cracked legs had been untidily repaired. I assumed Tucker had no carpentry skills.

I seated myself gingerly on one of the chairs, hoping it wouldn't collapse, but it held steady. Calum retrieved the container holding the ale.

"Do ye have any cups to drink from, Tucker?"

"Aye, yer lairdship. I set a few of the servants' cups and plates by." The butler retrieved two cracked porcelain teacups from a built-in wooden shelf above the hearth. I noted several plates as well.

"Get yerself a cup as well, my auld friend," Calum said.

Tucker froze, then turned to look at Calum with a heartrending expression of grief and love. I was left in no doubt that these two men had a relationship of long-standing and mutual affection.

"Thank ye, yer lairdship," the butler said. He set three cups on the table before turning back toward the hearth to put a pot on an iron frame over the growing fire.

Apparently, Calum and Tucker had gone to the same culinary school. I watched as the butler threw in the same ingredients that Calum had for his delicious stew.

Calum poured ale into the cups, and I sipped at mine. I would have killed for a glass of water, but I wasn't sure what I could and could not drink. Clearly, I didn't have the immunities to bacteria that Tucker and Calum probably had.

"Is there any chance you have some tea lying around?" I asked. "Maybe some boiled water?"

Tucker dipped his head in a nod. "Aye, madam. I do have some tea. Would you prefer tea to the ale?"

I gave Calum a sheepish smile. "Yes, please."

Calum took my cup and poured it into his.

"More for me," he said with a lift of his lips.

Tucker opened up a wooden barrel and scooped what I assumed was water into a smaller pot, which he hung over the iron tripod next to the stew. He then opened up a tin container and scooped out something that looked like tea leaves, placing them into the pot.

Turning to me, he shrugged.

"They took the teakettle and the stove."

Calum looked toward a large empty space along the wall.

"Aye, so they did," he said in a bemused voice. "A wonderful cast-iron piece from Glasgow. My mother loved it."

"That she did, master. I was ever so sad to see it go."

Calum and Tucker talked at length about the house and the surrounding tenant farmers, many of whom had apparently managed to keep their lands because they'd had no sons to send to Culloden with Calum. Most of those who had been of age and physical capacity had followed Calum. Tucker noted that the few who had not died on the battlefield had fled to the Colonies.

Calum fell silent. I hadn't known him for long, but the grief and guilt on his face was palpable, heartrending.

"Ye canna blame yerself, yer lairdship. The lads made their own choice to go. Ye didna force anyone."

"They would no have gone if I didna ask, Tucker." Calum finished off his ale and poured himself another drink.

"Aye, yer lairdship." Tucker turned away and stirred the stew.

My heart ached for Calum.

"Miss Brown is from the Colonies," Calum said after a while.

Tucker, ladling stew into several bowls, looked over his shoulder toward me.

"Ye never say!"

"Aye," Calum said with a nod. He didn't explain my presence any further.

Tucker set out some of Calum's oatcakes and served the plates of stew. He poured me a cup of tea and apologized for having neither sugar nor milk, neither of which I took anyway.

"That's fortunate then," he replied. He retrieved some spoons from the shelf and set them by our plates before seating himself.

"I apologize, yer lairdship, but they did take all the linen."

Calum sighed heavily. "My mother's Irish linen."

"Aye."

I watched as Calum toyed with his food, apparently having lost his appetite.

"You need to eat," I said firmly.

He looked up at me, his expression somber once again.

"Aye," he said, but continued to toy with his food. Frankly, he had seemed happier up in the hills, and I wondered if returning to the remnants of his ancestral home had been a good idea. But I was following him. I had no idea where to hide out in eighteenth-century Scotland.

I could have guilted and manipulated him into eating by suggesting that we needed his strength to survive, that I was totally dependent on him, but I opted to keep silent. I ate Tucker's equally delicious stew with relish though. The tea was interesting—stout, hearty and hot, but at least it wasn't ale. Ale for breakfast, lunch, dinner and snacks just wasn't going to work for me or my liver.

We finished the meal silently, and Tucker rose to clear the table. He cleaned the dishes and spoons and pot while Calum finished his ale and I drank my tea.

"I think Miss Brown needs to rest, Tucker. Did the merchants leave any of the bedroom furnishings?"

Tucker turned, his shoulders sagging.

"Nay, verra little, my laird. They took everything of value but left a few beds in the servants' quarters. Ye are welcome to take my bed. I can make do down here in the kitchen with a blanket."

"Nonsense, Tucker. I would no take yer bed. Let us go see what we can salvage. Perhaps we will join ye in the servants' quarters."

"Aye, yer lairdship." Tucker picked up the lantern and led us back through the great room and across the courtyard to a small doorway that led to a curving stairwell. We climbed and climbed and climbed until we reached what was, in fact, the fifth floor, which led to a hallway of about five or six small wooden doors.

I noticed on the journey that Calum hesitated on several of the floors, as if he wanted to look in on them, but thankfully he pressed on. I wasn't sure how much more loss he could handle in one day.

On arriving at the top floor, Calum looked around with interest. Had he never been up there before?

"These are all servants' quarters? I didna ken we had that many servants."

"Oh, many more, my laird. This is just...*was* just the household staff. The kitchen staff had their own rooms, the stable lads had their own room, the gardener, others."

"Aye, of course," Calum said in a bemused voice. "The estate agent saw to much of that. Do ye hear from Mr. Ferguson?"

"Nay, yer lairdship. Not since he returned to Ireland after the Crown told him to leave Scotland."

Calum nodded. "He was a good man." He opened the door of the first room and peeked in, withdrawing his head quickly.

"Forgive me, Tucker. This must be yer room. Could you show us to a room suitable for Miss Brown?"

"Certainly, my laird." He moved down the hall and opened a door.

Calum stepped inside the room, and I followed, feeling like I needed to sidestep to get the bulk of my skirts through the doorway. There was no room for Tucker to enter, even had he wanted to. Calum was not a small man, and his bulk took up much of the small room, which featured a low-pitched roof and a tiny iron-barred window at the apex of the pitch.

"It is a wee room," Calum said, looking around, "but I suppose it will have to do since there is a bed."

We looked down at the bed, larger than a twin but smaller than a double. A wooden chair rested next to the head of the bed, and a small cupboard sat next to that.

"Well, it's definitely larger than the room at the inn," I said, probably only by about two square feet, but I was trying to take a positive spin.

"I have some blankets set aside," Tucker said, "and I will bring up some hot water with which to wash." He reached into the cupboard and pulled out a worn and plain porcelain washbasin.

"The sun will rise soon, Tucker," Calum said. "Ye must be tired. I will see to our needs."

"Och, nay, yer lairdship. I dinna feel tired. I slept before ye arrived."

Calum nodded and turned for the door. Out of curiosity, I followed Tucker and Calum into the next room and looked in. Calum's room mirrored mine exactly.

After voicing his approval, Calum suggested I rest in my room while he and Tucker retrieved the necessary items to make the rooms hospitable. I watched them go and turned to look under the bed, looking for the one thing I was going to need to make the room hospitable—a chamber pot.

To my rising anxiety, I found none. What was I supposed to do? Descend five flights of stairs and go where? Out of the castle? The thought of asking Calum for a pot made me queasy. As it was, even if I did find a chamber pot, I was going to have to ask someone where to empty it. There was no way I was going to allow the old butler to carry my bodily waste up and down stairs.

I opened up the cupboard to see if anything else was stashed inside. With a sigh of relief, I withdrew a cracked porcelain bowl that resembled the chamber pot at the inn. Luckily, the crack was along the rim and not at the bottom of the bowl. I carried it over to the bed and stuffed it underneath, vowing to use it once everyone had retired for the night.

As I waited for Tucker and Calum to return, I imagined a scenario in which I pulled Tucker to the side and asked him discreetly how to empty the pot.

The window, high on the wall, called to me, and I climbed up on the bed to stand and peek out. The darkness had lightened, and I had a spectacular view of the mountains we had descended, the valley and part of the lake fronting the castle. The entire panorama was dressed in varying shades of the blues and purples of approaching dawn as the earth rotated toward the sun.

"Can ye see the loch?" Calum asked quietly behind me. I turned with a start and stepped down from the bed. Calum cradled some blue cloth in his hands, much like that of his plaid kilt. He set one blanket down on the bed.

"Yes, it's beautiful, just beautiful." I pressed my lips together before I said anything that might add to his grief.

"I remember the view from my room. I will no step on yer bed to look out though."

Tucker followed him in, toting a pail of hot water in one hand and what looked like linen over the other arm, with two bars of soap in his hand.

"Here ye go, madam," he said, setting down the linen and soap on the cupboard. Calum grabbed the bucket of water from him and poured some into the bowl.

"Yer lairdship! I can do that!"

"As can I, Tucker. And more easily than ye." He set the bucket down on the floor.

Tucker shook his head and left the room with the rest of the linen and soap.

"Ummm...Calum," I said. "I found the pot." My cheeks flamed. I wasn't sure why. I had, after all, made a big deal of going in the woods.

"The pot?"

"The chamber pot?"

"Ah!" Calum replied. "Aye, of course."

"Well, where do I empty it?"

He blinked and regarded me with surprise. "Och, I ken Tucker will perform that service."

"No! I don't want an old man hauling my...pot around. I can handle it. Where does it go?"

"What do ye do in yer time?"

"We don't. We have running water. It just goes away down pipes and off to the city to treat."

Calum was about to ask something else when Tucker returned.

"Do ye need anything else, yer lairdship? I regret there are no fireplaces in the servants' quarters. I hope ye will be warm enough."

"Will ye be comfortable, lass?" He turned to Tucker. "Perhaps we shall transport the beds down to the family quarters tomorrow."

"I'm fine. Ummm, Calum?"

He looked at me and followed my eyes to the floor by my bed.

"Ah! Aye, Tucker. Where do ye dispose of..." He jerked his head in the direction of the floor.

"I beg yer pardon, my laird?" Tucker looked confused.

"The...em..." Calum waggled his eyebrows. "The pots, Tucker. The chamber pots."

"Och, my laird. I will see to that in the morn."

Calum turned to me.

"There ye have it, lass. Tucker will see to it."

I rolled my eyes and took a deep breath, hoping the burning of my cheeks didn't show.

"Okay, okay," I said, throwing my hands up. "Thank you, Tucker."

"Of course, madam." Tucker bowed and left the room.

"Will ye be all right, lass?" Calum asked as he bent to pick up the hot water.

"Yes, thank you, Calum. I'll be fine."

"Sleep well." He turned and left the room, shutting the door behind him. Thankfully, predawn light filtered in through the window because I didn't think anyone had left me with a candle and whatever one used to light candles, certainly not matches.

I climbed up onto the bed to look out again. Purple had turned to orange and pink, as the sky now glowed with the sun that would soon rise over the mountains. The view was glorious, and I wished I had my camera. But that was long gone, as was my safe and secure life in the twenty-first century.

CHAPTER TEN

I thought I must have slept for only a few hours when I heard a commotion in the hallway. I awakened, sitting up in bed, having opted not to remove my clothing. I had wanted to be ready to run or hide if we needed to.

The sound of men's voices laced with a couple of curses and some sort of scraping sound brought me out of my bed. Since I was fully dressed, I had little to do but stick my feet in my shoes before hurrying to my door and looking out.

Calum and Tucker struggled with a small bed, which I assumed was Calum's. No lightweight steel rails—the frame was made of thick, solid wood.

"Good morn, lass," Calum said, setting his end of the bed down while Tucker followed suit. My heart went out to the butler. His skinny chest heaved, and sweat beaded his forehead and trickled down the side of his face into his scraggly white beard.

Calum, on the other hand, looked fit and hardy.

"I fear we awakened ye," Calum added. "Did ye sleep well?"

"Yes," I replied. I stared at the bed.

"We are moving the beds down to the family quarters, where there are fireplaces. Now that ye are awake, we can move yer bed as well."

I looked at Tucker again.

"I'm not sure Tucker can handle this," I murmured. "Why don't I help?"

"Nay, madam! I may be auld, but I can still do my chores." Tucker's expression showed righteous indignation, and I hurried to make amends.

"I'm sorry. Yes, of course."

Tucker looked hardly mollified as he made a point of picking up his end of the bed again.

Calum smiled, seeming to be in a better mood that morning.

"Nay, lass. I would no have let ye carry the bed either. Tucker brought some hot water and set it in my room. Get yerself some water, and wash up if ye like. Tucker and I will return for yer bed and furnishings."

Calum picked up his end of the bed, and the two men moved off in a shuffle down the hall toward the stairs. I had no idea how they were going to get the bed down the narrow spiral stairwell, but I wished them well.

After negotiating with my skirts to perform the necessary, I stuffed the chamber pot back under my bed with a wince and went over to Calum's room to find the bucket of water that Tucker had brought up. The water was still warm, and I carried it back to my room, poured some into the basin on the cupboard and washed my face and hands.

I returned the bucket to Calum's room just in time to see the two men emerging from the stairwell. Tucker's reddened cheeks attested to his exertions. Calum looked as if he'd done nothing more strenuous than carry a pillow downstairs.

"I will put ye in my mother's room. Ye will be comfortable there."

"Oh!" I said, standing back as he and Tucker stepped into my room to pick up my bed.

"Thank you," I said.

"It is next to mine and has a bonny view of the loch. I hope it will please ye," Calum said, picking up the foot of my bed.

"Oh, I'm sure it will," I said. Calum and Tucker struggled through the door with my bed, and I contemplated the absurdity of a mythical eighteenth-century Highland aristocrat handling furniture like Luigi, the moving guy.

I followed them downstairs this time, occasionally taking a seat on the stone stairs to wait while they negotiated two flights on the steep stairwell. Calum took the brunt of the weight at the bottom while Tucker basically pushed.

I learned a lot of Gaelic curse words, mostly from Calum, but I didn't commit them to memory, as I had no idea what they meant. The pair emerged onto the third floor and carried my bed down the hall and through an open door. I peeked in and saw a room devoid of furniture, draperies or decorations. The wooden floor held no carpeting, and the wood-paneled walls held no tapestries or art. The room looked barren with the exception of the small bed that Tucker and Calum set against a wall.

A large stone fireplace took up one wall and was flanked by two shoulder-height barred windows. I moved over to the windows to look out. Calum was right. The room did hold a beautiful view of the lake. I had not seen the lake during daylight hours, and I marveled at the beauty of the castle reflected in the still water.

Calum appeared at my side.

"I told ye it was a bonny view."

His presence, so close to me, reminded me of our long journey the night before, when he had held my hand the entire time. It felt only natural that I should lean into him and press my head against his chest, but I fought the urge. Holding my hand while we traveled through the dark had been the act of a considerate gentleman, not that of a man who was particularly attracted to me.

For my part, the Scottish laird fascinated me. He was everything I thought a Highlander should be, if I'd really given them any thought in the past—tall, broad shouldered, brawny and darkly handsome with a delightfully sensuous way of speaking English in his brogue.

I was sure that I was a curiosity to Calum, perhaps even fascinating in my persona as a time traveler, but I doubted that my fairly ordinary looks and unremarkable background elicited the same romantic feelings that he now stirred within me.

I cleared my throat and slipped out of his aura, moving away from the window.

"Yes, it is a stunning view. No wonder someone built the castle here."

Calum turned away from the window as well. "Och, the original tower house was built on the loch as a defensive measure against other clans. My ancestors added to the castle over the years—the barmkin surrounding the courtyard, which housed barracks for clansmen to fight against invaders, as well as the stables, brewhouse and bakehouse."

"Oh, really? So the castle wasn't this big when it was built?"

"Noooo," he said in the charming Scottish way. "It was just a wee thing."

"A wee thing," I repeated with a smile. "A five-story tower house."

"Aye, verra small, as castles go."

"How long ago was Castle Heuvan built?"

"I believe the tower house was built in about 1485 or thereabout."

I drew in a sharp breath.

"That's over five hundred years ago in my time."

Calum eyed me.

"Does it still stand in the twenty-first century? Do ye ken?" he asked in a hushed voice.

"I don't know, Calum, but I'm no expert on Scottish castles. If I ever get back one day, I'll make sure I become an expert though."

Calum tilted his head. "Get back. Do ye still ken it is possible to go back?"

I turned restlessly to look out the window again. "I don't know, but I should probably try to find out someday."

"It is no safe for ye to return to the river. The soldiers are looking for ye."

"Yes, I know."

Tucker entered, toting the chair from my room. "I ken I will need help with the dressers, master."

"Aye, of course, Tucker." Calum turned to me. "Ye are probably hungry. Tucker, ye said ye have some breakfast and a pot of tea set by for Miss Brown?"

"Aye, master."

"Why do ye no go down to the kitchen and have something to eat, lass? I will join ye shortly when we have finished moving the dressers."

I nodded and made my way down the spiral staircase to the small entryway that led out to the courtyard. I had just stepped outside, when I heard a short burst of banging nearby, as if a knock on a door, albeit loud.

My heart pounded as I rounded the base of the tower house and peeked around the corner. The large wooden door in the castle wall reverberated with banging.

Soldiers! They had found us! I ran back into the tower house and hustled up the spiral staircase, skirts pulled almost up to my waist. To my dismay, I didn't find Tucker and Calum until I reached the fifth floor. Panting and out of breath, I braced a hand against a wall to drag in some air.

"Lass! What is it?" Calum called out as he dropped his end of a dresser and hurried to my side. I gasped out my words.

"Knocking at the door downstairs. I think it's soldiers. I don't know. But someone's there."

Calum drew in a sharp breath and threw a look at Tucker before rushing into one of the rooms and peering out the window. As tall as he was, he didn't need to stand on one of the beds, as I had.

"I canna see who it is, Tucker. Were ye expecting someone?"

"Nay, yer lairdship. No one comes here except the soldiers."

"It must be the soldiers!" Calum said. "I did suppose they would follow us here if they discovered who I was. They wasted no time following us."

"Let me go down and see who it is, yer lairdship. Ye and Miss Brown can hide in the servants' quarters. The soldiers will no come up here. They never do, having grumbled in the past that it is too arduous of a climb. They havena returned to check those rooms since the first time they came. If they wish to stay, as they often do, they can bed down in the barracks on their blankets. I will bring food and drink to yerselves. It is too bad that we just moved the beds though."

"Aye, I should have waited to do such," Calum said. He wrapped his arm around me, and although I was terrified, his embrace reassured me.

"Go now, Tucker. We will await ye here."

Tucker hurried away, and Calum turned me to him, placing his hands on my shoulders.

"I canna tell ye dinna fash, lass, for we may be in a predicament, but I promise that I will do my best to keep ye safe."

I wanted to wrap my arms around his sturdy body, to bury my face against his chest, but I clenched my fists and nodded. To my surprise, he pulled me into his arms and rested his chin on my head. I heard his heart beating, loudly, a little fast. I gave in then and did what I had only dreamed of. I wrapped my arms around his waist, burrowing into the safety of his embrace.

"All will be well, lass," he whispered. "I promise."

Music to my ears. I wasn't sure Calum could promise that exactly, but I didn't care. I loved his words.

We waited for Tucker, not knowing if the soldiers were going to charge up the stairs. There were no back stairs, no other way out of the tower house. My body trembled with mounting anxiety, and Calum continued to whisper against my hair, holding me close.

Footsteps sounded in the stairwell, and Calum drew in a sharp breath, his already tense body poised as if for flight or fight.

"My laird, it is I, Tucker," the butler called out. He reached the top floor, slightly out of breath. "It isna the English, but I think ye must come down."

Calum relaxed, loosening his hold on me.

"Who is it then?"

"Come down and see for yerself, master." The butler turned and headed back down the staircase.

With an impatient sound, Calum released me and moved away to follow in Tucker's wake.

"Stay here, lass," he ordered.

"Not a chance," I muttered. I hurried after him. He paused at the entrance to the stairwell.

"Will ye no do as I say?"

"No, I don't think so. I'm coming with you," I said firmly.

He sighed heavily and started down the stairs. I followed closely. We reached the courtyard in a few minutes and rounded the tower house. Tucker waited at the closed door.

"Who is it then, Tucker? Why ye must be so mysterious, I canna imagine."

Tucker pulled open the door. I gasped. Outside the door stood a group of men, women and children, at least twenty or more. The men bowed. The women curtsied.

"My laird," a tall, thin elderly man said. "Welcome home." I heard further cries of "welcome" and "my laird" from the group. Tucker stood back, and they started filing into the courtyard.

Calum looked stunned. He stared as one by one, the men and women took his hand and bowed over it.

"Ye look bonny, my laird," one plump older woman said. "We thought ye dead at first when ye didna return from the battle at Culloden."

"Tucker! Shut the door!" Calum found his voice, albeit husky.

He turned to the group.

"Forgive me," he said to them. "I could no come home. I am a wanted man."

"Och! We ken that, yer lairdship!" the old man said. "The soldiers stop at my farm regularly to ask about ye, if I have seen ye, if I ken where ye were. But it were months afore we heard ye were still alive. We didna ken if we would ever see ye again."

"The soldiers will come for me," Calum said. "I am meant to be in hiding, not having guests for dinner."

I noticed curious eyes staring at me. I moved to stand behind Calum, as if his bulk could hide me. He looked over his shoulder at me, seeming to understand.

"This is Miss Brown," he said.

There were murmured greetings of "Miss Brown" and "yer ladyship," which I wasn't.

"Have ye fared well?" Calum asked the group. "Have the soldiers treated ye well? I have looked over the valley over the past year and have seen that the crops did well. Do you prosper?"

"The Crown requires us to turn most of the profit over to them, but aye, we are doing as well as can be expected," the older man said. "Feeling the loss of our lads."

Calum's shoulders sagged, and I realized the "lads" must have been killed at Culloden.

"Forgive me," he said. "Ye canna ken how I grieve for ye, for my part in taking yer sons and brothers wi me." He turned to the old man. "Robert Anderson, it was yer James who saved my life and pulled me wounded from the field to hide me in the trees."

"Aye, so we heard from two of the lads who returned. They said James died from the wound of an English sword."

"He did." Calum nodded, grief ravaging his face. "He saved me, but I could no save him."

A murmur of mutual sadness moved through the crowd.

"Ye said two of the lads returned," Calum said. "Who?"

One of the women spoke, middle aged, plump, with gray hair peeping out from a white cap.

"My lads, Robbie and Andrew. They escaped from Scotland though and have gone to the Colonies. I dinna ken if I will ever see them again." Her voice cracked, and she dashed at tears that slipped down her face.

"Robbie and Andrew. Aye, I remember the lads. So, they have gone to the Colonies. Have they written?"

"Aye, I had a letter some months ago. They found some farm work in a place called Massachusetts."

Calum looked over his shoulder at me before turning back to the crowd.

"I have heard of Massachusetts," he said. "Ye have another lad home with ye, dinna ye, Flora Anderson?"

"Aye, my son, Niall. He's near fifteen now. Tends to the farm, though he wants to join his brothers."

Calum sighed heavily.

"I have naethin left to give ye, but if there is aught I can do for ye, please tell me."

"Nay, yer lairdship. We havena come to ask ye for aught but only to welcome ye home," Robert Anderson said. I noticed everyone seemed to have the same last name. I supposed that had something to do with the clan system...or maybe they were all related. However, they were Andersons, and Calum was a Campbell.

"I would offer ye some food and drink," Calum said, "but I dinna think Tucker has much set by."

"No need, my laird," Flora said. "If ye are in need, we can provide the house some food from our stores."

Calum shook his head.

"Nay, I canna accept. I ken ye are stretched thin yerselves, from what the Crown leaves ye. I thank ye for yer visit. Please dinna speak of my presence here."

"Aye, yer lairdship." Robert turned and shepherded the group back out through the gate. "It is so good to see ye home, my laird," he said before turning away.

Tucker shut the door, and to my surprise, Calum sagged against the wall. He pressed his head against the stone and closed his eyes.

Tucker and I exchanged a glance, but we said nothing. That Calum grieved was evident. A vein throbbed in his temple, as if he fought strong emotion.

With effort, he pushed away from the wall and turned to us.

"I wish with all my heart that I could go back in time." As if he realized what he said, he looked at me, startled.

"Lass," he began.

"What?" I asked. "How?"

We both looked at Tucker.

"Tucker, would ye please boil up some tea for Miss Brown? We will follow ye to the kitchen shortly."

Tucker, looking from one of us to the other in some confusion, turned and hurried across the courtyard.

"If *I* can't travel back through time, how can *you*?" I asked with a shake of my head. A small part of my brain noted that if Calum *could* travel back through time, where would that leave me?

"I dinna ken that I could, lass, but if I could, if it was possible to save the lives of my men by not taking them into battle, should I no try?"

Chapter Eleven

"What are you suggesting? That we go back to the river and see if you can travel back in time? You can't pick and choose what time you travel to! What if you ended up in the twelfth century or something?"

Calum seemed to give that some thought, thankfully.

"Och! I didna think of that. But ye tried to travel back to yer time. Why did ye think ye might return to the twenty-first century?"

"I don't know. I just assumed I would go back to the same time. I didn't choose to travel through time, and I certainly didn't choose to travel to the eighteenth century. It sort of picked me. I don't know why I'm here."

"No, I canna imagine why either. It seems as if ye must be here for some purpose though. Else why did ye no travel to the twelfth century yerself?"

I shrugged.

Calum took my hand and tucked it under his arm.

"Let us go eat some breakfast. I am no finished with this conversation."

My heart dropped as I allowed Calum to lead me across the courtyard. I couldn't imagine the consequences if he could travel in time, because I was absolutely sure he wouldn't end up exactly where he wanted to…or when…and what would happen to him then?

We ate largely in silence while I stared at Calum trying to read his thoughts while he stared at the fire. When he had finished eating his porridge, he leaned back and looked at Tucker, who had declined to eat but was stirring something in a pot.

"When does the regular patrol of English come again, Tucker?"

Tucker turned, wooden spoon in hand. "Could be on the morrow, yer lairdship. They came on Tuesday last week."

"That is if they dinna arrive today," Calum added. "I thought surely they must have discovered who I was and followed in our wake here to Castle Heuvan."

"Why do ye think they kent who ye were? Did ye give them yer real name?"

I swung my head to look at Calum. "Your real name?"

Calum's cheeks bronzed, and he blinked and looked away.

"Nay, I didna. But I sensed Lieutenant Dunston suspected who I was. I didna tell Miss Brown my real name either, but I suppose I must now."

Tucker ducked his head and returned to cooking what I presumed was lunch.

I returned my attention to Calum...or whoever he was.

"Well, what's your name then?"

"Malcolm," he said. "Malcolm Anderson."

"Malcolm Anderson," I murmured. "So that's why all the Andersons."

"Aye, I am an Anderson. Calum is the Gaelic version of Malcolm. My mother was a Campbell. Her clan fought with the English, so I used that name when the lieutenant asked who I was."

"But I thought your mother—" I stopped.

"Aye, it was as I said. She hated the English, would have hated to ken that her kin fought with the English."

"So what is your official title then?"

"I am the Earl of Luckland."

I quirked an eyebrow.

"An earl?" I said in an impressed voice.

"In name only. And someday soon, I expect the Crown will give that title to someone else, someone loyal to the English, just as they may give this castle and my lands to another."

He ran a hand across his dark beard and looked toward the fire once again. From the way he chewed on his lower lip, I knew he struggled for control of his emotions.

"So, shall I call you Malcolm or Calum?"

"I will answer to whatever ye wish to call me," he said, returning his gaze to me. A small flash of white teeth told me he had put his grief aside for the moment.

He pushed back his chair and rose.

"Let us finish moving furniture, Tucker. If ye say they are unwilling to climb the tower house stairs, then the family quarters will be just as safe as the servants' quarters."

"Aye, yer lairdship." Tucker moved the pot off the hottest part of the hearth and followed Calum—for I continued to think of him as Calum—

out of the kitchen. I swigged down the rest of my tea and followed, unwilling to be left alone in case someone else came knocking on the door...like the English.

I was of little help in hauling furniture, but I did convince Tucker to let me carry pillows and blankets. I offered to empty the pots, but Calum put a stop to that.

"Ye shall no carry mine anywhere!" he said decisively. "Tucker will tend to them."

And that was just as well. I didn't want to deal with Calum's waste. That was way too practical and earthy for such a handsome, mythical man.

I wondered again how I was going to manage in the eighteenth century. Would I get used to the lack of plumbing? Of central heating? I hadn't told Calum, but I'd been very cold in the night, and although I'd pulled my icy feet close to my body, they had never truly warmed up.

I eyed the large fireplace in his mother's room, relishing the idea of having a fire during the night. I made the beds with the limited linens and blankets while Tucker carried away the washbowls and chamber pots. Calum stood by and watched me.

"I ken I must go to the river, lass. I must try."

I whirled around, already on edge because he'd warned me he wasn't done with the subject.

"Calum! It can't work. I think the results would be disastrous for you!"

"But surely ye see that I must try? I have no life here, lass, no home, no lands. It matters little if I dinna return. Had I kent that the river had such special properties, I would have dunked my head in it long ago."

His words hit me like I'd been punched in the stomach. I opened my mouth to scream at him. *What about me? I love you. Why would you leave me alone here? What do you mean you have no life here? What about me?*

But the words choked in my aching throat. I couldn't speak. I pivoted back to the bed and smacked the blanket, as if to straighten it.

"Lass?"

I was afraid I would break down in tears if I spoke. I took a deep breath, gritted my teeth and eked out a few words.

"I won't help you."

"I am no asking ye to help me, lass. I remember where we stood in the river. I remember that ye splashed water on yer face. I dinna think there is much else to ken?"

"I'm not helping you, and I think it's a stupid idea. But that's your business."

Why didn't he understand that he would leave me stranded if he left? I knew no one except him. Where would I go? What would I do? How would I find him in time again? I had suspected he didn't feel the same about me as I did him, but did I mean so very little to him that he had no regrets about leaving me…or trying to leave anyway?

But I remained silent. I wouldn't ask him the questions. I understood he wanted to assuage his grief, to bring back to life the young men he'd led to their deaths at Culloden. I could never understand the depths of his guilt and grief, but I understood that he grieved.

I turned, and unable to meet his eyes, I walked past him to look out the window onto the valley.

"I must go before the soldiers come," he said. "I dinna fear they will find me here in the castle so much as I dinna wish to encounter them on the way back through the hills to the river."

He came to stand beside me as I stared down at the lake, its calm waters mirroring not only the castle but the surrounding hills.

"I must go tonight," he said. "The more I think on the matter, the more I ken I must try, and that I must go soon. Seeing the families of the lads was almost too much to bear."

Tonight? Another sharp pain seized my stomach. I wanted to argue with him, but it seemed pointless.

"Do what you think you need to."

"Ye sound angry with me, lass. Ye have said that ye dinna wish to help me, and for that I am thankful. It would be too dangerous for ye to accompany me. If I can find my way back in time to stop our failed march on Culloden, then I will return to the castle. I dinna ken how it might work, but if ye awaken tomorrow morn and discover that yer room is filled with furniture, ye will surely ken that I succeeded."

I shook my head and turned my shoulder. There was no way it was going to work, and I was mostly likely having my last conversation with Calum ever…if he managed to travel back in time. If not, the soldiers would find him, and they would eventually discover who he was.

I wasn't sure what I thought Calum should do with the rest of his life. He couldn't hide out in his old castle forever. In fact, it sounded like some new occupant might come to claim the castle any day. I had no idea how arduous a trip to the United States was in the eighteenth century, but I felt that might be Calum's best chance to survive.

I heard Calum sigh, and then he moved away. I wanted to grab his hand, to throw myself in his arms and beg him not to try to travel in time, but I didn't. He left the room, and I let the hot tears slip down my cheeks as I hugged myself tightly.

I brushed at the tears and did my best to stop them. Unsure of what to do with myself, I sat down on my bed, leaned my head against the paneled wall and closed my eyes. I tried to think of anything but Calum and his plans. I imagined us on a picnic by the shores of the lake. I must have dozed, because a tap on the door awakened me. Tucker, carrying an empty chamber pot and washbowl, entered the open door.

"Forgive me, madam," he said. "I didna ken ye were resting. I will just set these down and leave."

"Thank you, Tucker," I said tiredly.

"I have some the rest of the stew boiling in the kitchen if ye're hungry," he said, bending to slide the chamber pot under the bed.

"Thank you, but I'm not hungry."

"That's all right then, madam. The food will be ready when ye are. I will leave ye in peace now."

He closed the door, and I shut my eyes again, wondering dully what Calum was doing. What did one do in a castle all day?

I fell asleep again, and I awakened some time later, chilled. I opened my eyes to see the room in shadow, as if it was late afternoon. I gasped and sat upright, having never intended to sleep the day away.

Why hadn't Calum awakened me? I jumped off the bed and hurried to the door. He probably hadn't awakened me because I'd been angry with him. I pulled open the door and hurried to his room. No one answered my knock, so I turned and headed for the stairwell. I made my way down to the ground floor and across the courtyard to head for the kitchen.

On entering the kitchen, I saw no sign of Tucker or Calum. The fire burned low, and two pots hung on the rack. One of them I recognized as the pot of water for tea. An empty plate and teacup, spoon, tin of tealeaves and a plate holding several oatcakes awaited me at the table.

"Hello?" I called out. "Tucker? Calum?" I waited to hear a response, but none came. I stared down at the table again, guessing that Calum had already eaten lunch. By the dimming light coming through the single window in the kitchen, I wondered if it was almost time for dinner.

"Calum?" I called again. "Tucker?" I crossed the room and lifted the wooden bar on a door to peer outside. I wasn't surprised to find the back door of the kitchen led to yet another part of the cobblestoned courtyard. I noted an open wooden building that resembled some kind of stables, though I heard no horses.

"Calum?" I called out. I waited, but no one responded. I shut the door and turned around, wondering where they were. With a sigh, I picked up the plate to carry over to the hearth.

A piece of paper, thick and off white, tucked under the plate caught my eye, and I grabbed it. The handwriting, in an elaborate cursive style, was difficult to decipher. I didn't even recognize some of the letters, and I had to guess at several words.

Ye slept so peacefully that I didna...to wake ye, lass.

I have returned to the river. Tucker accompanies me. I didna wish him to leave ye alone at the castle, but he persuaded me that it would be best if the two of ye...what happened to me in the event that I succeed or dinna return.

I hope that yer anger with me has...somewhat. I was saddened by yer displeasure and dinna wish to disappoint ye again.

Tucker will return to care for ye in my absence. Should I no be able to return, please avail yerself of the castle as long as possible. I gave Tucker what little money I had, which will see ye through at least a year. Hopefully, I will return long...then, and all will be right with the world.

Calum

By the end of the letter, it didn't matter that I couldn't decipher some of the script, because I was crying too hard to see the writing.

Calum had gone without me! He had left without telling me, and I had no idea how long he'd been gone. He could have left hours ago. I looked at the fire. Maybe he and Tucker had left only moments ago.

I jumped up and ran out of the kitchen, through the great hall and across the courtyard to wrestle open the heavy castle doors. I peered out onto the valley and lake, glowing now in shades of lavender and blue as the sun sank below the hills. I saw nothing and no one, and I slammed the door shut and ran into the tower house to climb the stairs to my room. Panting for air, I looked out the window and scoured the countryside but saw no one. From this viewpoint, I could just make out the faint light line of the trail that Calum and I had followed in the night to reach the castle.

Something broke the linear streak of the trail, something dark. Cattle? Sheep? Not boulders. The trail hugging the hillside had been free of boulders. No, the figures moved, two of them. They headed up into the mountains, away from the castle.

Calum and Tucker! It had to be them. I whirled around, my first instinct to run after them. I flew down the stairs, and taking no time to grab anything to drink or eat, I returned to the door in the castle wall and pushed through it. I grabbed my skirts in both hands and trotted down the trail heading for the hills, hoping that the moon would be full that night. I would have killed for a flashlight.

Calum and Tucker had long ago disappeared from view. I found the trailhead and began the climb. Flat ground soon fell away, and my heart pounded with a combination of effort and fear. I clutched my skirts in my left hand and thrust out my other hand to steady myself along the hillside to my right.

Night had fallen in earnest, but the moon, large and round, shone down on me, making the trek a little less worse than it could have been. I climbed for at least an hour, my throat raw from gasping for air. I desperately missed Calum's arm around my waist and his strong hand pulling me along behind him.

As I scrambled up the hill, a sound caught my ear—male voices. But the cacophony told me that there were more than two men. The voices were not those of Calum and Tucker. I froze, listening to the loudest voice, an obviously irritated man.

"And look! Night has fallen, and it's dark as pitch. It's taken us twice as long to get down the trail than usual. Why we couldn't just get some sleep and make for the castle in the morning is beyond me. Very convenient for the lieutenant to return to Fort William with his coughing spell. I suppose he'll be sleeping good tonight."

"Pipe down, Hancock! I be mighty tired of listening to yer grumbling. We know this trail well enough. It ain't the lieutenant's fault he's a sickly sort. I don't know how he got a commission."

"Pipe down yerself, Buford. I'll grumble all I like. And he got a commission because he's gentry, that's why. Not as if the likes of us could ever get a commission."

"At least the sergeant didn't abandon us."

"No, he'll be bringing up the rear."

I snapped out of my frozen posture, realizing that the voices were just around the corner, and I threw myself onto the hillside and clawed my way up the hill, digging my fingers and toes into dirt and grasping at whatever shrubs I could feel. My skirts dragged at me, my feet slipped, and I heard stones fall to the path.

I froze at the clatter of the stones and looked down. I'd only made it about fifteen feet up the hillside. The men came into view, highlighted under the moon. I dug in my toes, plastered myself to the side of the hill, held my breath and wished with all my heart that I hadn't left the castle.

I didn't recognize the soldiers as those whom Calum and I had escaped from, but they all looked alike to me in their uniforms—the red and white now appearing a ghostly blue and black at night. The soldiers *had* mentioned the lieutenant, so I assumed they were the same group, albeit fewer men than I remembered. I was too scared to count the soldiers, alternatively peeking over my shoulder and slamming my eyes shut while I hoped they didn't see me. They didn't have Calum and Tucker in tow, so it seemed they had bypassed the men in some way.

I hoped that the clever sergeant "bringing up the rear" wouldn't look up and spot me. If anyone was going to find me, it would be him.

The group shuffled tiredly past me, and sweat dripped down my forehead onto my nose as I held on to a couple of shrubs. They moved out of sight, and I waited with aching arms until I could no longer hear their steps before I slid back down the hill to the trail. I paused and listened carefully. It was always possible that more men followed. I heard nothing further, and I allowed myself a single strangled sob of terror before turning and hurrying up the trail again.

Picking up my pace to put distance between the soldiers and me, I scrambled noisily over the occasional loose stones. I knew I should have been quieter, but I had no chance of catching up to Calum and Tucker if I didn't hurry.

I should have taken my time and been more cautious. That was what I told myself when an arm caught me from behind and a hand closed over my mouth.

CHAPTER TWELVE

"Lass, dinna scream. It is I, Calum," a familiar baritone whispered in my ear.

I tore at his hand and whirled around, unsure of whether to smack him or hug him. Tucker stood behind him.

"Stop doing that!" I hissed in a low voice. "Sneaking up on me and clamping a hand over my mouth!"

"Forgive me, but there are soldiers on the trail now on their way to the castle. Did ye no pass them? How is it they didna see ye?"

"Because I climbed up the hill when I heard them," I grumbled, still trying to calm my nerves down.

"Why did ye come, lass? Did ye no get my letter?"

I nodded, eyeing him in the moonlight, my handsome Highlander. A warm sensation filled my heart, no doubt replacing the adrenaline that now retreated.

"I did, but I wanted to go with you," I said simply.

"Go with me? Ye dinna mean through time, do ye?"

"Tucker," I murmured in warning.

"Och, I have told Tucker everything, else he would have been wondering what our journey was about."

"Well, I meant I wanted to go with you to the river, but now that you mention it, maybe go with you through time...if we can." There was always that caveat...if we can.

"I dinna ken," Calum murmured with a shake of his head. "As ye said, lass, it is dangerous. If I can return in time, I might go too far."

"Or you might go forward in time...to my time. You'd be lost there without me, Calum. It would be so difficult for you."

Calum took my right hand in his and lifted it to his lips. The warmth of his lips and tickle of his mustache and beard made my heart jump before it started to beat erratically. I tried to pull my hand away, but Calum held it firmly, if gently.

"I think I might be lost without ye anywhere, lass," he murmured.

My knees weakened. I didn't even care that Tucker cleared his throat and looked down at the ground.

"I can't bear to let you go, Calum. I can't lose you," I whispered.

"And I canna bear to say good-bye to ye." He bent his head to mine, pressing his forehead against my own, cupping my hand between us and laying it over his heart.

I closed my eyes and felt his heart beat—strong and steady. I tried to hear his thoughts but could not.

"I have to go with you," I whispered.

"Aye, ye must," he said somberly. "As long as we are together, everything will be all right, *mo chridhe*. I will no lose ye, and ye will no lose me."

He raised his head and kissed my forehead before lowering my hand, though he kept it in his own. I didn't know what he had called me, but I hoped it was a term of affection.

"Shall we go then?" he said, the flash of his teeth sweet in the moonlight. He led me back up the trail, Tucker taking up the rear. We crested the hills and reached the meadow near Calum's cottage. He avoided that side of the valley and kept to the tree line on the opposite side, saying we could disappear into the trees should more soldiers appear.

He said he had recognized some of the English soldiers as those who had taken us prisoner, but he had not seen the lieutenant. He wondered whether they were still in the area or whether they had returned to Fort William.

"I heard the first two soldiers talking. They said the lieutenant returned to Fort William with a coughing spell. And that the sergeant was in the rear of the formation."

"I would no wish a man ill, but it is just as well the lieutenant returned to the fort. He was particularly fervent in his desire to capture a rebellious Scottish laird. And a strange lass from the Colonies."

We reached the far side of the valley, and Calum paused before we began our descent.

"Do ye need to rest, lass? We have some oatcakes and ale."

I shook my head.

"Not unless you two do. I'm okay."

"I am no tired," Tucker offered.

"Verra well then. It is just as well that we dinna stop. We may yet encounter more soldiers."

We started our descent down into the river valley. I wasn't sure how long we'd been traveling, but I guessed it was about two and a half to three hours. Calum supported me with a strong arm as we followed the steep trail, this one through the trees but not as treacherous as the one clinging to the side of the mountains near his castle.

"Ye did well, lass," Calum said in a hushed voice as we emerged from the trees into the river valley. "I ken the journey must have been challenging in yer gown, even as fetching as it is." He pulled my hand to his lips again and smiled quickly, sending chills up and down my exhausted spine.

"This way," he said, leading us out onto the trail through the valley. The moon, thankfully still bright overhead, highlighted the path. Now that we neared the river, dread set in, and I clung to Calum's hand with a tight, emotional grip. My throat ached, and I didn't know how to deal with my anxiety. Either Calum would travel or he wouldn't. I was going with him one way or the other.

We reached the river all too soon, and I'm afraid I dragged on Calum's hand a bit as I tried to slow us down. Selfishly, I hoped he wouldn't be able to travel through time without me. I hoped that I would be able to travel through time with him. I hoped and wished that the events that had taken his land, home and people from him could be resolved. The chaos of my emotions, of my hopes and wishes, made me dizzy.

"We are here," Calum said.

"Close," I said.

"Then we must go to the verra spot where you first arrived. Lead us."

But it was Calum who had to pull me along the river path until I thought we reached the location where I had first awakened in eighteenth-century Scotland.

"Okay," I said, coming to a halt. "This is it."

"Are ye certain, lass?"

I nodded.

"Verra well then." Calum turned to Tucker and put a hand on the old man's shoulder. "I dinna ken whether I will see ye in a few moments, a few days or a few years, my auld friend. Ye mean a great deal to me. Stay well. I ken ye have made plans to move in with yer daughter should the British boot ye from the castle, so I have no fears for ye on that account."

"I dinna truly ken what ye are about to do, yer lairdship, but I wish ye well. I have loved ye like a son." Tucker's voice broke, and he turned to me quickly.

"If I dinna see ye again, madam, farewell." He bowed.

Calum cleared his throat and took my hand. He turned toward the riverbank and led me to it. I heard the sound of the rushing water with dread. What would happen in the next few minutes? There was really no good outcome, as far as I could see.

If Calum and I could not travel to another time, we would probably have to leave Scotland. If we traveled back in time, I seriously doubted we would travel to the perfect time for him, before he made the decision to join the Jacobite rebellion at Culloden. If we traveled forward in time, we could very well end up in an era neither of us had connection to—the future for him and perhaps still historical for me.

"Yer hand is shaking, *mo chridhe*."

I nodded and grabbed the chance to ask him a question I might never be able to ask him again.

"What does *mo chridhe* mean, Calum?"

He brought my hand to his lips.

"My heart, for ye *are* my heart, lass. I love ye dearly. Are ye ready?"

I nodded, bemused by his declaration of love and wanting to throw myself into his arms. I didn't want to leave this moment, not ever.

"What if this doesn't work?" I said fretfully. "What if we do nothing but get our faces wet?"

"I have given that a great deal of thought, lass. In the event that I fail to turn back time, I think we must make for the continent, perhaps Rome, Paris?"

"Oh!" I said. "Rome! I've been to Rome. Let's do Rome." I tried to smile, remembering the calendar shot I had done there some years ago.

"Rome then," Calum said. "I do hope yer Italian is better than mine."

I managed a chuckle before tightening my grip on his hand.

"Don't leave me," I whispered.

"Never."

We knelt down on the bank.

"Scoop up the water with your left hand," I said, "and I'll grab some with my right. Splash it on your face. That's all I can think of. I'm not sure this will work, but if it does, I have no idea what's going to happen."

"Dinna let go of my hand, *mo chridhe*."

"I won't. Are you ready?"

"Nay. Aye." Calum pulled my hand to his lips for a quick kiss.

"On the count of three," I said. "One, two…" I swallowed hard.

"Three!"

We bent over in unison and scooped water out of the river, splashing it on our faces. Calum held my hand in a vice grip. I gasped at the icy water. My face tingled.

Chapter Thirteen

I opened my eyes to daylight. Lying on my back, I noticed that the sky was gray, overcast. It could have been early morning, midday or late afternoon. I had no idea.

Calum!

I pushed myself upright and looked around.

"Calum!" I screeched, panic rising. "Calum!" I leaned forward and searched the river. Had he fallen in? The current wasn't really strong enough to carry him away. He didn't lie facedown on the bank anywhere.

I stood on shaky legs.

"Calum!" I shrieked. Tears flooded my eyes, blinding me. I rubbed my eyes and whirled around, blurrily scanning the landscape for any sign of Calum.

"Calum!" My throat closed over, making it hard to call out to him. "Where are you?"

I looked down at my left hand, staring at the appendage as if it were evil. Had I let go of him? Where was he? Where was I? That some hours had passed was evident because it was daytime.

I continued rotating, searching for him as if I was on some sort of tilt-a-whirl park ride.

"Calum!" I continued to call, my voice raspy, tears flowing unchecked.

I had lost him. I had lost him, and I didn't know where he was. I didn't know where to go, how to find him, what to do.

I looked at the river and threw myself back down onto the bank, recklessly splashing water on my face. I didn't care where I ended up so long as it was with Calum, wherever he was.

Nothing happened. No tingling. No swirling darkness. The icy water did nothing but cool my heated cheeks. I sank back on my bent knees and stared at the hills above the river. Burnt orange dotted the hillside, suggesting that it was still fall. Had Calum traveled in time, but not me? If so, where had he gone? I hoped and prayed he had not gone to the twenty-first century. He would be so lost there. It hurt to picture my brawny Highlander reduced to the frailty of little more than a defenseless child, and I couldn't rid myself of the image.

"Calum," I called out weakly, by now expecting no answer. There was no way on earth he would have simply walked off and left me. None.

I suddenly remembered that Tucker had been standing behind us, and he was missing as well. Sweat broke out on my upper lip as I realized it was probably I who had traveled in time. But to what year?

I pushed myself up again and studied the path paralleling the river. It seemed very similar to the road in the eighteenth century—wide and rutted from wagons. I distinctly remembered the trail in the twenty-first century had been no more than a footpath without signs of wheeled traffic.

I wondered if I should head for the village and risk capture by the English soldiers, at worst, or being seen by the landlady, at best—and then turned over to the soldiers. Or whether I should head another way. I gave myself a shake, trying to remind myself that I had traveled through time. I had no idea if English soldiers were after me or not.

The journey back to Castle Heuvan would take a long time, but I had to know where Calum had gone, if he had achieved his dream to travel back to a time before Culloden.

I struck out down the road, heading for the hills, and steeling myself for the ascent. If I had only traveled through time a few days one way or the other, then it was still possible the soldiers would be on the lookout for me...and for Calum.

I hadn't walked far when I saw a figure astride a horse heading toward me. A soldier! I panicked and dove headfirst into the brush, as I had so long ago...or only a few days ago. I covered my head with my hands and hoped the rider hadn't seen me.

The slow but inexorable thud of hooves grew louder, the volume echoing my heartbeat. Foolishly, I hoped the rider couldn't hear it. The brush was golden, and I wasn't sure my drab-gray clothing could camouflage me effectively.

The horse stopped, and I almost screamed with anxiety and fear. I rotated my head slowly to peek at the rider. A Highlander sporting a gray tam over shoulder-length curly black hair gazed down on me from his big brown horse. Clean shaven with an angular face and firm chin, he was as handsome as Calum. He sported a knee-baring kilt and black riding boots. Tilting his head to the side, he eyed me curiously.

"Lass, what are ye doing hiding in the brush? Are ye hiding from me?"

I pushed myself up on my elbows with flaming cheeks and met his gaze.

"Well, yes," I said. "I thought you might be the English."

"The English? Do ye mean soldiers?"

"Yes, soldiers." I said no more but rose to a sheepish standing position.

"Are ye in need of assistance, my dear? Ye canna be in a verra good spot if ye are hiding from soldiers."

I studied him carefully. What could you tell about a person by just looking at him? A gold wedding band showed on his left hand. At least this Highlander was truly married.

"Well, I could use some help. I'm kind of lost."

The Highlander's chin lifted, and he stared hard at me for a moment. My heart thudded again. What had I said?

He threw a leg over his saddle and slid down.

"Aye, I can see that ye are. Are ye a time traveler?"

My jaw dropped, and I sputtered.

"Wh-what? No! What? Time traveler? Hah! No!"

What was happening? How could he possibly know? No one had ever traveled through time, to my knowledge, not really. How could a man in the eighteenth century just grab that idea out of thin air?

He put a hand to his chest and spoke in a soothing voice.

"I can see that I have scared ye, lass. Ye have no need to fear me. My name is Colin Anderson. My wife comes from America, as I think do ye."

"Yes, I'm from America. That's right!" Relief flooded through me, but on the next breath, I wondered why. Even if his wife was American, she came from a different time than I did. I would be just as strange to her as I was to any Highlander. What were eighteenth-century American women like anyway?

I almost missed the fact that he said his last name was Anderson. Almost.

"I was just on my way to the village, but if ye have nowhere else to go, I think I must turn around and take ye to her. Even if ye do have somewhere else to go, I should take ye to her. She would be most pleased to make yer acquaintance. Perhaps she can explain a few things to ye. Perhaps ye can explain a few things to us."

"Well, I'm sure I don't know what to explain to you. Oh, yes, maybe the hiding-from-the-soldiers thing. Yes, that. That's weird, I know."

"Ye can explain that to me as we ride."

"So I'm just going to get up on the horse with you? Just like that?"

Well, of course I was. I had few choices.

"Aye. We will keep ye safe from the soldiers, that I promise."

"Oh! Okay!"

Colin climbed back up on his horse and leaned down to grab my arm.

"Put yer foot on mine and swing yer limb over the horse's back. If ye're who I think ye are, ye willna mind riding astride."

Who did he think I was? I did as he said and found myself sitting on the back of a Highlander's horse. Colin looked down at my athletic shoes, and I did my best to push the hem of my skirts down over them, with little luck.

"I recognize those shoes. Aye, ye and my wife will get along verra well, my dear."

I wanted to know what he meant, but he turned the horse around and changed the subject.

"Now, what is this about the soldiers? How did ye run afoul of them?"

I bit my lips.

"Did you say your name was Anderson?" I spoke to his broad back encased in a thick black coat.

"Aye, Colin Anderson, at yer service."

"Are you any relation to a Malcolm Anderson?"

Colin pulled on the horse's reins, bringing us to a stop. He turned and looked at me with slate eyes.

"Malcolm Anderson? Do ye mean Calum? How do ye ken Calum?"

Again, relief flooded through me. Yes! He knew Calum!

"Is he like a cousin or something?" I didn't answer his question directly.

"Aye, Calum is kin."

"Oh, thank goodness! How is he? Where is he? Do you know?"

"I dinna ken where he is." Colin tightened his lips, turned around and urged his horse forward. I had the distinct impression he wanted to end that line of questioning. I didn't care though. I pressed on.

"Where is he?"

"How do ye ken Calum?" he asked.

"It's complicated," I said. I wasn't actually sure I could trust Colin, cousin or not.

"Why is it complicated?"

"Well, how do you feel about him?"

"What a strange question, lass! I might ask the same of ye."

"I love him." There, I'd said it out loud. I loved him. Not that it was doing me much good at the moment.

"Please tell me what you know about him, where he is," I begged.

"I dinna ken how ye came to fall in love with my cousin, but the last I saw of him, he was doing well."

"Where is he?"

"Lass, I canna tell ye that."

"Please. I wish I could tell you how I know him, but I can't. He wouldn't mind if you told me where he was. We became separated."

"How?"

"I can't explain it to you."

I heard Colin sigh heavily.

"It seems we are at an impasse, my dear. I canna in all conscience discuss Calum's whereabouts with ye, as I really dinna ken ye."

I stared at Colin's back and took a chance.

"Okay, you're right. I've traveled through time...from the twenty-first century. Calum rescued me and took me to a cottage. I don't know if you know, but he's wanted by the British. They found us at the cottage and were about to haul us off to Fort William, but we escaped. He took me to his castle on Loch Heuvan. But the castle and lands were taken by the Crown because he participated in the Jacobite Rebellion. I'm sure you knew that.

"Calum regretted his decision to participate in the rebellion and to take some of his men with him. He wanted to try traveling back in time to reverse his decision to go to Culloden so that the men and boys could live. So we tried traveling back in time together. I woke up, and he was gone. I don't know if he traveled in time or where, and I'm not sure whether I traveled back or forward in time. What year is it?"

Colin looked over his shoulder at me.

"1747."

"What? 1747?" I racked my brain, but I couldn't remember the actual date that I'd traveled to other than it was 1747. I knew it was still fall or perhaps late summer.

"So ye are saying ye lost Calum? In time?"

"I don't know...I don't know," I muttered. "This is going to sound so stupid, but I had no idea what the date was. I knew it was around fall of 1747, but I didn't know the exact date. It's not like there are a lot of calendars posted to walls. How will I know where Calum is? How do I know if *I* traveled in time and he didn't?"

"I last saw Calum almost a month ago at the cottage. I stopped by to see how he fared."

"Oh! That's a while ago! So we still don't know where he is or what happened to him or, frankly, who traveled in time."

"I wish I could help ye, lass, but I dinna ken how."

"I don't know either," I murmured, tempted to lay my face against his broad back and cry. I resisted the urge.

"I'll have to go up into the hills to the cottage to see if he's still there." At some point, I noticed that we didn't cross over the river to turn toward the hills but continued to follow it. "How far is it to your place?"

"No far at all. Ye may no ken, but the cottage is on my land. It is an abandoned sheepherder's cottage. My own herder, Duncan, has another cottage in the hills closer to my house."

"Calum said it belonged to a cousin of his. I heard the sheep at night," I said.

"Aye, they are noisy enough, noisier still when Duncan brings them down from the hills in the winter to graze near the parklands."

"Parklands?" I repeated absentmindedly. My attention was almost entirely focused on how to find Calum.

"Aye, the lands surrounding my house."

"How long would it take for me to get from your house to Calum's cottage?"

"Hours! And a great deal of climbing. I canna let ye go alone though. I will go wi ye."

"Can we go today?"

I hated to see Colin shake his head, but he did.

"Och, noooo, lass. It is much too late to undertake such a journey. Ye will come to the house first and meet Beth. We will leave first thing in the morn."

"Is Beth your wife?"

"Aye."

Exhaustion swept over me without warning, and I rested my head against his back. I felt an arm come around me as if to keep me on the horse, and I fell asleep.

Chapter Fourteen

I awakened to the feel of strong hands around my waist, pulling me downward. I thrust my arms out to stop my fall, only to discover upon opening my eyes that Colin was pulling me from his horse. He set me down on the ground in front of him and placed steadying hands on my shoulders as I weaved slightly.

"Ye fell asleep," he said.

"I did, didn't I?" I smiled faintly. Turning, my eyes bulged as I caught sight of his house, a stunning gray stone mansion flanked by castellated turrets. A well-kept lawn, falling away into forest, surrounded the massive house. The parklands, I presumed.

Colin caught my eye. "My home, Gleannhaven Castle," he said simply.

A large oak door opened, and a petite woman came running out followed by an elderly man who moved more slowly. Two black-and-white sheepdogs followed them. The woman stopped short and stared first at me, then at Colin. Dressed in a beautiful gown of rose silk with an embroidered underskirt, she wore her auburn hair piled high on her head. Could this be Colin's American wife?

"Colin? Are you serious?" she asked, her accent definitely American. If I hadn't been so flustered, I would have realized that the phrase she used was distinctly modern.

"I am, my dear. Please allow me to present my wife, Lady Elizabeth Anderson," Colin said, taking his wife's hand and pulling her forward. He blinked and laughed. "I am ashamed to say that I didna ask yer name. How is that possible?"

"Lily Brown," I said, staring at the couple.

"Lily," the woman repeated softly. She took my hand in hers and looked up at her husband. "Did you find her by the river?"

"Aye, my dear, that I did, hiding in the brush."

Elizabeth turned back to me with wide eyes.

"Oh boy, I'll bet there's a story there!" She looked down at my dress. "Well, thankfully, I'm going to guess that you've been here for a while and know that you've traveled in time."

My jaw dropped, and I looked from Elizabeth to Colin and back to his wife again.

"You?" I gasped. "Really?"

"Yes, me too," Elizabeth said. "Come inside and tell me what happened to you." She pulled me by the hand and led me toward the house. A young teenage boy ran up from around the side of the mansion and took the horse from Colin.

I followed Elizabeth through the door, the dogs running ahead of us. The older man bowed as we passed, and I guessed he was a servant rather than a family member, probably the butler. Colin brought up the rear.

I was flabbergasted by the sight of a castle in its prime. Unlike Calum's home, this castle was fully furnished, warm and well lit. Elizabeth led me down a hallway and into a room decorated in rose and green tones. Similarly colored silk, velvet and brocade furnishings softened the gray stone walls, and carpets covered the wooden floor. A large white-mantled fireplace dominated one wall of the room. The dogs preceded us into the room and settled themselves at the foot of various chairs.

Elizabeth settled me onto a velvet rose sofa and turned to the elderly, wispy-haired servant who had followed us in.

"Some tea, please, George."

"Right away, yer ladyship," he said in a thick brogue before leaving the room.

Elizabeth turned back to me.

"Well, tell me all!"

An hour later, I had learned that she had been called Beth Pratt before she married the Earl of Halkhead, that she was from the twenty-first century and from Montana, which she said, on a chuckle, was not a wee village south of Boston. I assumed from the look she and Colin exchanged that they had an ongoing private joke about that. She told me that I was now the third time traveler in the area—all of us having been women from the twenty-first century. The other woman was named Maggie Scott, and she had married a delightful Highlander named James Livingstone, and they lived not too far away at Castle Lochloon. She said she and Colin had a three and a half month old baby, also named Elizabeth whom they called Lizzie, and who was currently napping.

As we exchanged information, Beth gestured for silence when the butler returned with a serving girl named Grace to deliver the tea. Beth poured for us, and we resumed our discoveries about each other. I told her that I was a photographer from the Seattle area, shooting calendars, and that while some friends would notice I had vanished, my parents had passed away, and I was an only child.

"Why do you think we traveled in time?" I looked from Beth to Colin and realized how insensitive that must have sounded. "Well, I can see why you traveled through time, Beth, but what about me? Surely other women have splashed water on their face near the river. It's a popular hiking trail."

Beth looked at her husband and raised an eyebrow.

"Well, I have my theory," she said. "I don't know why we were 'selected' to travel back in time, but I think we were destined to find love...and that love just happened to be in the eighteenth century."

The intimately tender glance that passed between Beth and Colin made my heart flutter.

"And you've fallen in love with Calum, haven't you? I can hear it in your voice."

"Yes," I said. "I have, wherever he is."

"Well, I'm glad. He's a good man. Terribly sad but honorable. So where is he? Where could he have gone?"

"We journey up into the hills tomorrow to see if he is at the cottage," Colin said. "Miss Brown wishes to see for herself."

Beth nodded.

"I've climbed those hills a time or two myself. I know how rough they are, but I understand that you want to see if Calum is up there for yourself."

I sipped on my tea and stared down at the carpet for a moment before raising my eyes.

"I'm not sure I have any hope of finding Calum up there, and if I do, won't that mean that he won't have met me, that he won't know who I am?"

Again, Beth and Colin exchanged glances. I was getting used to it.

"That actually happened to me. I didn't tell you that I traveled back to the twenty-first century again...just for a moment, mind you, but I did it to change something that happened in the past." Beth bit her lip and shook her head. "No, that doesn't sound right. What I mean to say is that I traveled forward in time and then managed—and I still don't know how—to travel even further back into the eighteenth century to try to save Colin's life." Her voice grew husky, and her cheeks reddened.

"I really can't say much more about it, and I don't even know if that's helpful. Maggie traveled back to the twenty-first century to get medicine for James, who was ill. It almost seems as if we can travel again to reach a time to help the men we love." She looked to Colin as if for verification, and he nodded thoughtfully.

"Aye, my love, I believe ye have something there. The question is, does Miss Brown attempt to return in time yet again, or does she have purpose in our time?"

"It's mind boggling," I said. "I still don't know what the date was when I first arrived...or even now."

"It's the 17th of September, 1747, if that's at all helpful," Beth said with a sympathetic droop of her lips.

"September 17th," I repeated. I shook my head. "No, nothing comes to me. I guess I never asked Calum what the specific date was. I knew it was fall from the colors of the landscape, and he told me the year was 1747, but that's about it. I guess we'll find out tomorrow."

"Unless Calum isn't there," Beth said. "I don't mean to state the obvious or make you sadder than you already are."

"No, you're right. Calum might very well not be there. I'm not sure what I'll do then."

"You mean whether you'll try to go back to the twenty-first century or not?"

I shrugged and swallowed hard. Go back forever?

"I'd have no chance of finding Calum if I went back. No chance at all, unless I try to find some historical reference to him." A lump formed in my throat, and I couldn't continue the thought.

Beth reached over and patted my hand.

"You'll find him somehow, I suspect," she said with an attempt at a reassuring smile. "You don't have to decide anything today. You and Colin will look for Calum tomorrow, and depending on what you find out, you can make a decision then. You're welcome to stay here, Lily, as long as you need to. I'd love the company."

I curled my fingers around her small hands.

"Thank you, Beth. Thank you both." I forced a smile.

"Now, how about a bath? I'm not saying anything, but I'll bet you're dying for a hot bath, aren't you? And a change of clothes? We're about the same size. I can loan you a few things. Dresses, of course, but..." With a deliberately cheerful smile, she let her words trail off.

I pulled up the hem of my skirt and couldn't help but grin.

"Oh, look at you!" Beth crowed. "Smart girl! You can't wear them in public, but hey, jeans!"

Colin coughed and turned away to finish off his tea. He rose.

"I have some paperwork to attend to at present and must leave ye ladies to yer pleasures." He bent and kissed Beth on the forehead before leaving the room. Beth rose, and I followed suit.

Thanks to Beth, I enjoyed a lovely hot bath in a beautifully decorated room with a roaring fire. I suspected that Beth was giving me the royal treatment with the addition of the midday fire due to my twenty-first century sensibilities.

She returned to the room following my bath, with a change of clothing—a lovely thick bodice jacket of hunter green and a woven skirt in a solid shade of dark blue. She gave me fresh undergarments as well, all of which fit very well.

Beth laughed when she looked at my shoes.

"Oh, gee, yes, I showed up in my athletic shoes as well. Too funny! You'd better keep those. They're really going to be much more comfortable than anything I could give you."

She helped me dress my hair, twisting it up onto my head in a soft coil before securing it with some hairpins, while telling me about her baby, Lizzie, who was at present in the nursery with the nanny.

"She's adorable. She doesn't really do much yet, but she smiles now, even laughs a little. Or maybe it's gas—who knows!" Beth grinned. "She has black hair and dark eyes like Colin."

Beth gave my hair a last pat and twirled me around in front of the mirror.

"I decided to give you something sturdier to wear since you're going out with Colin tomorrow. I would rather have dressed you up in something silk or satin, but this is more practical."

I looked down at my bodice jacket and skirt.

"Oh, these are beautiful, Beth, really?"

"Yes, they are. I know the clothes in the eighteenth century are kind of fussy, but you'll get used to them."

She looked up at me and scrunched her nose.

"Oh, I'm sorry. I mean if you stay, if things work out."

I nodded with a lopsided smile.

"I know what you mean. I don't care where Calum is. I just want to find him."

"I understand," Beth said softly. "Come on down and let's have tea. Early supper to you and me." She chuckled. "I'll introduce you to Lizzie."

We descended the stairs, and Beth tucked her hand under my arm to lead me to what she called the great room. Massive oak beams highlighted the ceiling and matched the wood of a long rectangular table in the middle of the room. A large stone fireplace flanked one wall, and it was in one of a pair of high-backed velvet chairs fronting a toasty fire that Colin sat holding a little baby. Behind him, the butler and several serving girls moved about laying food out on the table.

Colin saw us enter, and put a finger to his lips.

"She has just fallen asleep…again."

Beth pulled me forward.

"She likes to sleep," she said with a grin. "Well, you won't get to meet Lizzie right now exactly, but you can see her anyway."

I loved babies, and peeked over Colin's arm to ogle the sleeping infant wrapped in a soft-appearing white blanket. She slept peacefully, her cherubic little face serene. She looked healthy.

"She's beautiful," I said to the preening parents. Beth blushed.

"She looks like Colin," she said. "Beautiful black curls and black eyes." Beth ran a tender hand along Colin's hair before he caught it and brought it to his lips. My heart melted. I hadn't had the opportunity to touch Calum as they touched each other, and I worried that I might never get the chance to run my fingers through his hair, to caress his forehead, to feel the pulse at the base of his throat.

I worried I would never feel his arms around me again, as I had all too briefly.

A young woman in a white linen cap and pale-blue bodice and gown entered and approached us. She eyed me curiously while dipping a quick curtsey

"Ah! Bridget, Lizzie has fallen asleep again. Back to the nursery she goes." Colin rose and handed the baby to her. The nanny, I presumed.

"Aye, yer lairdship. She is a good sleeper, is this one. My wee sisters and brothers all slept verra well too when they were bairns." She looked down at the baby and smiled before offering her to Beth, who kissed Lizzie's forehead.

"See you, baby," Beth said. Bridget left the room with Lizzie in her arms, and we turned toward the table.

Supper was delicious, and I could see what I thought were some modern touches in the food, courtesy of Beth, but I was completely distracted by thoughts of our journey to find Calum in the morning. I could hardly remain silent, as I was the guest of honor, but even Beth could see that I was worried, and she allowed me to finish the remainder of my meal in silence while she chatted with Colin about Lizzie, the estate and whatever else a mixed twenty-first century and eighteenth-century couple talked about.

We drank tea after dinner in the lovely rose and green drawing room, and then went away to our respective rooms for the night. Beth offered me a maid to help me undress, and I declined. She seemed to understand.

A fire burned low in my room, keeping the chill away, and my bed had been turned down. Candles burned on a table by the bedside. A fresh white linen nightdress invited me, and I shrugged out of my clothes and into the nightgown. I slipped between the sheets and contemplated the following day, my thoughts nothing but a chaotic jumble of hopes, wishes, fears and apprehension. Only one thing was clear to me. I had to find Calum. I had to find him.

Chapter Fifteen

Colin and I set out early the next morning with Beth waving us off and calling out words of caution and encouragement. The dogs jumped around at her heels as if they were going on the trip, but Colin told them they had to stay home. They sat down obediently, if a little wistful.

"It will take you a few hours to get up to the hills, maybe another to cross over into the other valley where Calum's cottage is," Beth said. "I've actually never been there. I hope you find him, Lily. I really, really do. Colin will get you up the hill. I'm sorry you have to wear the dress, but you never know when you might run into some soldiers. Colin will hide you if he hears them."

Some wonderful maid had taken my clothing to clean them overnight, and they were in good shape. I didn't want to try another dusty journey in Beth's lovely blue skirts that I'd worn the previous day. Beth had pressed a dark cloak upon me, insisting that I would need it if I got cold. She tied it around my neck. I didn't really want the extra weight, but I couldn't very well refuse her.

The climb began in the hills rising from the parkland directly behind Gleannhaven Castle. Much steeper than the climb through the other hills, I heaved and gasped, the cloak dragging me down, my skirts pulled almost to my throat as Colin hauled me up. He clearly had some experience dragging women up and down the hills, and as we climbed, he told me about meeting Beth and their subsequent adventures.

As Beth had said, the climb took several hours—or so I guessed, still lacking a way to tell time—and we crested the hill to see a meadow similar to the one where Calum had been living. My heart, already racing from the climb, jumped. The view was so similar that I almost imagined Calum walking up to me, the material of his kilt swaying against his knees.

But Calum didn't magically appear, and I swallowed my disappointment.

I noted Colin had worn trousers today, and I assumed the Highlanders wore trousers and kilts interchangeably, at least when out of sight of the English.

"Colin, why were you wearing a kilt yesterday down on the road leading to the village? They are banned, aren't they? At least, that's what Calum said."

Colin chuckled.

"Aye, they are banned indeed. I am cautious when I wear my kilt, but I am no a wanted man like Colin. If I am seen wearing my tartan, I might be inconvenienced with a fine. Calum disna need to flaunt himself as a rebellious Highlander. He already is one."

He took my hand to wrap around his arm for support as we followed a trail through the meadow.

"I dinna ken if we will see Duncan, my sheepherder. I think he must still be further up in the hills with the sheep. That is his cottage on the right."

I looked at the stone cottage, almost an exact replica of Calum's. Excitement made my heart bounce.

"What if Calum is in there? What if he decided not to return to his own cottage? Or..." I shook my head, confused. "I'm sorry. I don't really know what year he's in, so I don't know what to think."

Colin nodded.

"Aye, we should check the cottage. I dinna see smoke from the chimney, but it is a fair day."

We walked over to the stone cottage, and Colin knocked before lifting the latch of the door. I hoped and prayed and wished with all my might that Calum would come walking out when Colin pushed the door open, but he didn't. Colin looked inside and thoughtfully stepped back to allow me to peek inside. I did so with an ache in my throat.

As tiny as Calum's cottage, the layout was almost exactly the same. The hearth was cold, and the bed tidily made.

"He isna here," Colin said. "We should hasten for the next valley if we dinna wish to spend the night here in the hills."

I followed him further into the valley before turning left to head for a forested area. We walked through the forest, reaching a rise.

"The valley is just on the other side of this hill. Since I've neither heard nor seen any sheep, I ken Duncan must be further up in the hills. We should reach Calum's cottage in a short while."

We followed what was undoubtedly a sheep trail over a thankfully gentle hill and dropped down through the trees to within eyeshot of Calum's cottage. Upon seeing the gray stacked stones of the building, I quickened my step and left Colin behind.

"Wait for me, lass. Ye canna ken what is inside," he called out. I ignored him and ran up to the door of the cottage, pulling up the latch and pushing the door open.

"Calum!" I called out in a breathless voice. I stepped in and surveyed the room in shock. The bed had been overturned, the table legs broken, chairs smashed.

Colin reached my side.

"Who did this?" I whispered, appalled at the wanton destruction.

"I would assume the English did, perhaps in anger when Calum and ye escaped."

"Oh, gosh, that's right," I said. "I'll bet they were mad."

"There is nowt here that canna be set to right though. However, this disna answer the question as to where Calum might be. He isna here or he would have tidied up."

I shook my head, my shoulders heavy with dejection.

"No, he's not." I wanted to pick up chairs, to right the table and fix the broken legs, to tidy the bed, all so that the small cabin could be presentable when Calum returned. But would he return?

I turned to Colin and looked up into his sympathetic dark eyes.

"Where is he? Where could he have gone?"

Colin settled a consoling hand on my shoulder and shook his head.

"Come. Sit down, Lily. Let us have some refreshment as we think about what to do."

He took two of the chairs and set them outside the door of the cabin, then returned for two tankards. We settled down as if we were on a Colonial porch, and from the pockets of his coat, Colin withdrew a small bundle wrapped in cloth and a container of ale. He poured out the ale and offered me an oatcake. I sipped the ale and nibbled on the edge of the cake, with no appetite.

I had been forming a plan, and I wasn't sure if Colin would be on board with it. I didn't even know if it would involve an overnight trip, but I suspected it would.

I glanced at him out of the corner of my eye a couple of times but said nothing as I struggled to form a persuasive argument.

"What are ye thinking, lass?" he asked. His use of the word "lass," so like Calum, brought me near to tears.

"Me?" I stalled. I really didn't want him to shoot down my idea outright.

"Aye," he said with a half smile. He munched on an oatcake and watched me.

I drew in a deep breath and let it out.

"I want to go to Castle Heuvan," I finally said. I hurried to convince him before he could think about it. "I know it's a long way away, but I can't just go back without checking. You don't have to come with me. I know the way. I can go alone. And if he's not there, if nothing has changed, I'll go back to your house."

At some point, Colin had nodded, and I ignored it, so intent was I in my persuasion. He held up a hand.

"I have agreed that is the next logical step, my dear. Aye, of course we must go to Castle Heuvan."

"Oh!" I exclaimed, my cheeks flaming. "I'm sorry. I was so afraid to ask you. I know it's a long way."

"We are already here. It would be foolish to turn back when we have come so far."

"Good. Can we go now?"

Colin laughed, stowed the oatcakes and ale into his cavernous coat, and took the chairs back inside the cottage while I returned the tankards to their rightful place on the cupboard next to the fireplace.

We set out again, keeping to the edge of the tree line, as Calum had done. Colin seemed to know his way around the area well.

"I dinna ken if soldiers continue to frequent the area, but we must be cautious," he said.

"Yes."

We crossed the meadow in good time and paused for a moment to look down on the valley. A haze hovered over the lake, and we couldn't see the castle.

"Are ye ready?" Colin asked.

"Hold there," a voice called out from behind us.

I swung around with a gasp, pulling the hood of my cloak over my head. Colin stiffened and turned more slowly.

A small complement of English soldiers emerged from the trees, about ten of them. As they approached, I crossed my arms and slipped a not-so-casual hand across the lower half of my face. I lowered my eyes to the ground, hoping they wouldn't recognize me.

"Good afternoon, Sergeant Wilson. What brings ye to these parts?" Colin asked in a measured voice. I peeked up beneath my eyelashes. Yes, the sergeant was the same one from the pub, who had taken us captive at the cottage.

"Still looking for rebels, your lordship."

I listened to the conversation rather than watched, as I kept my eyes down. Colin must have felt the need to explain our presence.

"My wife's sister, an avid historian, wished to see Castle Heuvan, so I am taking her down to Loch Heuvan to see the castle."

"Is that so?" the sergeant said. I wasn't sure if I heard suspicion in his voice or not. Thank goodness the lieutenant had returned to Fort William.

"Aye, it is a bit of a strenuous stroll, but she insisted."

"She looks unwell. Are you ill, madam?"

I shook my head, then nodded.

"Aye, our journey took a wee bit longer than she expected, so we will stop to rest soon." Colin spoke on my behalf.

"We will move on then," I heard the sergeant say. "Madam."

I think he was saying good-bye. I didn't know, so I nodded again, keeping my arms crossed and my hand over my lower face.

I wasn't sure why the sergeant didn't recognize me, but he didn't, and none of his men called attention to me either. Out of the corner of my eye, I watched them file away, and I laid a shaky hand on Colin's arm.

"He was with the soldiers who caught us." I wasn't sure "caught" was the right word, especially for me. Calum had been caught because he'd been in hiding. What had they done with me? Taken me hostage? No. Captured me? Had I gotten loose like a hamster from a cage? Had they found me? Had I been missing?

"Aye, I wondered when ye covered yer face. He didna seem to recognize ye though."

"No. I'm not sure how, because he's pretty observant, but I don't think he did recognize me."

Colin turned to watch the soldiers cross the meadow and head into the opposite tree line.

"They have been patrolling these hills for over a year. Quite a nuisance. Calum managed to avoid them when they came. On several occasions, he escaped down to the valley to stay with us until my sheepherder, Duncan, reported the soldiers had left the hills. Ye say ye met him at the Blackbriar Inn. I did warn him to avoid that place, as the soldiers frequent the village on their way to and from Fort William. But Calum is a stubborn man, as ye may well ken. He claimed he tired of his own cooking.

"Perhaps we should sit for a wee spell until the soldiers are well and truly gone. If there is a chance that Calum hides in the castle, I wouldna wish to see the soldiers follow us."

I was anxious to get underway again, to get down to the valley, but Colin was right. He held out a hand while I lowered myself to a nearby boulder, and he took a seat beside me. I kept the hood of the cloak over my head and thanked Beth for the hundredth time, embarrassed that I had complained silently about wearing it.

"I have no cups," he said with a smile, pulling out the ale. "Do ye mind sharing?"

I shook my head and took a swig of the stout drink.

"Are ye hungry?"

I shook my head.

"No, just anxious to get down there." I looked toward the mist-shrouded area, unable to see either the lake or the castle.

"I ken ye are restless, lass," he said. He looked over his shoulder. "I still see some wee bits of red through the trees, though they are moving away. We can leave soon."

Colin gave it about five more minutes before he helped me to my feet. My heart raced. Would we find Calum at the castle?

We found the trail and began the descent. The mist closed in on us fairly quickly, necessitating that we slow down even more than the narrow trail dictated. I chafed at the pace but could do nothing to get us there quicker.

We passed no one on the trail, thank goodness, because I wasn't about to try scrambling up the hillside once again. Not in the thick mist. Occasionally, I looked out over where I imagined the lake and castle were, hoping for a break in the fog so I could see, but to no avail.

Eventually, the path leveled out, and I could see that we had dropped below the mist. The castle appeared before us, the lake beyond.

We followed the road leading to the castle. To my surprise, a wagon materialized in the distance, moving in our direction. I wondered if it belonged to one of the tenant farmers. Could it be Tucker?

I clutched at the hem of my skirts, probably for something to hold on to as I watched the approaching wagon with a mixture of excitement and curiosity.

"Who do you think it is?" I asked Colin foolishly. How would he know?

"I dinna ken," he said, taking my arm and leading me from the middle of the path. "We shall find out soon enough."

The wagon reached us, and I looked up at a young man with a freckled face and mop of red hair, who nodded and wished us a good day as the wagon, pulled by a large black horse, moved on. I stopped and turned to look at the wagon, which appeared to be empty. Something seemed odd about the scenario, but I couldn't put my finger on it.

"I wonder where he's going," I said.

"Perhaps to get some hay for the horses from a nearby field."

I nodded and turned forward.

"Well, let's go see what we can see!" I picked up my skirts and marched determinedly toward the castle, leaving Colin to follow. We reached the large double doors, and Colin banged on one of the doors with the side of his fist.

My heart pounded, my throat was dry, and I wavered on unsteady legs as we waited to see if anyone would answer. As an afterthought, I pulled my hood over my face again, with the thought that soldiers might open the door. Then I would never know where Calum had gone.

"Tucker must have come back here," I muttered. "I'm sure he'll come eventually.

"Aye," Colin said. He banged again. I wanted throw myself against the door and start pounding on it, but I resisted, instead locking my hands behind my back.

Finally, the door opened, and I stared at the fresh-faced young teenage girl gaping at us. She saw Colin and dipped a quick curtsey.

"Yer lairdship," she murmured.

"Have we met?" Colin asked.

"Och, nooo, yer lairdship, but I ken who ye are."

"How?"

"I've seen ye at the castle afore when ye visited with his lairdship."

"Is he here?" I burst in.

"Aye, madam. Come in."

I expelled a long breath that I didn't know I'd been holding, and my knees buckled. Colin grabbed me and pulled me upright. He half carried me through the door, and I came to a stop, transfixed at the scene.

The courtyard was a beehive of activity. Men and women crossed it, carrying baskets of cloth and foodstuffs, several barrels of hay, and other assorted items.

"What is all this?" I murmured.

"I dinna ken," he said. "I have checked on the castle several times over the past year, and it was largely deserted with the exception of Tucker, the butler."

"Well, I was just here a day or two ago, and it was deserted. I'm stunned."

The young woman beckoned to us, and we followed her across the courtyard and through the door leading to the great room. I assumed she was taking us through the empty room to the kitchen, but I drew in a sharp breath when I saw the great room.

"This isn't possible!" I breathed.

A long shining oak table dominated the room, flanked by about twenty high-backed oak chairs. Several buffets rested against walls, above which colorful tapestries and paintings hung. A fire danced in the large hearth.

At the head of the table, a man perused various papers while eating a solitary meal. He looked up when the door opened. So quickly did he jump up that he knocked his chair over. I barely recognized him. It wasn't Tucker.

CHAPTER SIXTEEN

Clean shaven, his dark hair well groomed and tidy, Calum hurried forward. He stopped in front of us and stared.

I couldn't speak. My heart was in my throat. I wanted to breathe his name, to throw myself into his arms, but I stood frozen, staring at the man in the tastefully embroidered brown velvet waistcoat, crisp linen neckcloth and well-cut dark-black trousers.

"Calum!" Colin said heartily, grasping Calum's hand and patting him on the shoulder. "Ye are alive and well!"

"Aye, cousin," Calum said, throwing a quick glance toward Colin before returning his gaze to me. Where had he been? I wanted to know so much about him, but when I opened my mouth, nothing came out. Nothing.

Where had he been? His hair was much longer than it had been, tied back at the nape of his neck with a black ribbon. He couldn't have grown his hair in the past two days.

He must have traveled in time. Did he know me? Did he recognize me?

"Calum, do ye recognize Miss Brown?" Colin asked. I was barely aware of Colin's presence by now.

"Aye," Calum said as if expelling a long breath. He took my hand in his, bent over it and pressed his lips to my skin. I stared, unable to understand who this version of Calum was. Was he a Calum from the future? The past? My head swirled. My knees threatened to give out.

The warm touch of his lips on my hand did nothing to bring me back to reality.

Calum straightened but did not let go of my hand.

"I have missed you, lass," he said in a husky voice. "I didna ken if I would ever see ye again."

At Calum's words, my heart jumped, pumping blood throughout my body. I ran into his arms, and he held me to him, murmuring unintelligible words against the top of my head.

I barely noticed that Colin moved away to settle himself at the table.

"I love you, lass. Do ye still feel the same about me?"

"Still?" I asked in a broken voice. I lifted my head to look at him, still staring at a clean-shaven stranger. His face was angular, his cleft chin firm, his lips generous and soft. "You've only been gone a little less than two days."

"Has it only been two days?" he asked. "Och, no, *mo chridhe*. I have been back here at the castle for almost a year. I have waited for you for a year."

"A year?"

"Aye."

Calum bent and kissed my lips. He pulled me even closer into his embrace, and I wrapped my arms around his neck, holding him to me. At the moment, I didn't worry about how he'd been gone a year. I didn't worry about Colin's presence. I didn't worry about soldiers and a Jacobite rebellion.

My head swam with the warmth of his lips, the pressure of his arms around my waist, the strength of his body against mine. I murmured his name over and over again silently. *Calum. Calum.*

A voice broke into our magical reunion. Colin asked the young maid who had brought us to the great room for some food and tea.

Calum lifted his head, stared at me hard, kissed my forehead and turned toward Colin, keeping my hand in his and leading me to the table.

"Please sit," he said almost formally, as if he spoke to a stranger.

I took a chair, wishing that my clothing was clean, my hair combed, my breath fresh. I feared I was a mess after our trek through the hills.

Calum touched my shoulder lightly before returning to his chair at the head of the table. He leaned his elbows on the table and stared at the both of us.

"How did ye come to meet Colin? How did ye ken I would be here? Did Lily tell ye about herself? About traveling through time? She tells me I have only been gone two days? And yet, I returned to the castle a year ago, before Culloden."

I stared at him, happy but confused. Colin did the talking.

"It is glad that I am to see ye, Calum. Glad indeed. Did ye say that ye had returned a year ago? Then ye did travel through time?"

Calum gazed at me with a look of such affection that my heart melted.

"Aye, I expect ye ken that Lily and I attempted to travel back in time together. My desire was to change the past, to ensure that I never encouraged the lads to accompany me to Culloden."

My eyes were glued to Calum. I studied the lines of his face, so unfamiliar to me. The touch of his lips on mine still tingled.

The door at the end of the great room opened, and Tucker appeared, followed by a young serving girl bearing a large tray. Tucker eyed me with surprise but said nothing as the tall blonde teenager set plates of food in front of us as well as a tea service.

"Tucker!" Colin said. "A pleasure to see ye."

"And ye as well, yer lairdship. It has been some time since ye were last here."

The serving girl left, and Tucker turned to me.

"Madam, it is so good to see ye, so verra good to see ye again." Uncharacteristically, he moved forward and took my hand in his. "We thought we had lost ye forever."

My face flamed, and I patted Tucker's hand.

"And I'm so glad to see you too, Tucker. You do know it has only been two days in my time since last I saw you, right?"

He shook his head uncomprehendingly.

"Nay, madam. Ye both disappeared nigh on a week ago. I didna ken where either of ye had gone, but I returned to the castle to find this!" He gestured toward the length of the great room. "The castle fully restored, his lairdship safe and sound, and all the lads alive and well."

He looked over at Calum, as if remembering his place, and he bowed again.

"I must return to my duties. So good to see ye, madam."

"You too, Tucker!"

I turned to Calum in confusion.

"But Tucker didn't travel in time, did he? He would have had to touch the water, wouldn't he?" I looked from Calum to Colin.

"No, he is the only one who didna travel in time. I have been without a butler for almost a year, but I kent that he would come back in September. It was ye that I fashed about, Lily. I kent ye did no come back with me, but I didna ken where ye had gone. Ye must have traveled only a few days forward in time."

I shrugged. "I really don't know. I didn't even know the date when I was here."

Calum reached over to take my hand in his.

"It disna matter, my love. Ye are here now."

"Tell us how this came to pass," Colin said, almost gesturing to encompass the dining room. "Castle Heuvan was naethin but an empty shell last time I saw it."

"I returned to a time before I convinced the lads to accompany me to Culloden," Calum said simply. "And kenning our fate, I dissuaded any who sought to march off to war without my consent, though I could no explain why I forbade it. A few grumbled, but most were content to stay home. Once they learned of the rout, they were grateful no to have gone into battle."

Calum released my hand and allowed me to pick up my cup of tea. I hadn't wanted him to let me go, but the table was large, and it had been quite a stretch.

"And as ye see, all is as it was. The soldiers come by occasionally to seek rebels, as they do on yer land, Colin, but I have no rebels hiding here."

Colin nodded and grinned.

"I am pleased for ye, cousin. This traveling through time is a marvelous thing, nay?"

"It is," Calum said. "Though I dinna wish to do so again." He glanced at me out of the corner of his eyes, as if he had a question.

"I didna ken a Scotsman could do such, but I think I willna give it a try myself," Colin said. "My lady and child are in need of me."

"I agree, Colin. It is naethin to be undertaken lightly."

Calum looked at me again. I could see that he did have a question.

"What?" I asked.

Calum toyed with a fork. I waited. Colin applied himself to his meal.

Calum looked over at Colin before turning to me.

"I dinna ken if ye are disappointed to remain in the eighteenth century or whether ye wish to return to yer time." He threw another look at Colin, who seemed increasingly intent on his food. "I dinna why ye traveled to the eighteenth century, lass, but I believe ye came for me. I believe ye came to live with me, to love me, to stay with me. I dinna wish to influence ye unduly to stay, but I love ye, and I will love ye for the rest of our lives, whether ye return to the future or stay with me."

The anguish in Calum's face tore at my heart. I loved him with more passion than I had ever known in my life, and I couldn't bear to see him unhappy. Now that he had regained his life and eased the burden of the guilt of Culloden, he should have been happy. Yet his eyes told me that he had suffered over the past year. He had loved me and lost me. He loved me still. I had no doubt what my response was, had been since the moment I met him, really.

"I'm staying with you…if you'll have me," I said.

Calum looked as if he was going to jump up from his chair, but he leaned forward and took my hand again.

"Aye, I will have ye, *mo chridhe*. I will most certainly have ye. Ye have captured my heart, and I dinna wish to be parted from ye ever again."

He squeezed my hand, his eyes shining. He threw an irritable glance at Colin then pushed back his chair, knocking it over, and jumped up.

"Och! I canna be bothered with ye and yer presence, Colin. I will embrace my lady." Calum moved swiftly to pull me from my chair and folded me into a tight, warm embrace. I pressed my face against his chest and listened to the strong and steady beat of my laird's heart.

Colin ignored us and ate.

ABOUT THE AUTHOR

Bess McBride is the best-selling author of over fifteen time travel romances as well as contemporary, historical, romantic suspense and light paranormal romances. She loves to hear from readers, and you can contact her at bessmcbride@gmail.com or visit her website at www.bessmcbride.com, as well as connect with her on Facebook and Twitter. She also writes short cozy mysteries as Minnie Crockwell, and you can find her website at minniecrockwell@gmail.com.

Made in the USA
Columbia, SC
16 January 2025